THE PILATUS
ENIGMA

THE PILATUS
ENIGMA

A Novel of Global Mystery and Murder

THOMAS W. BECKER

THE PILATUS ENIGMA
A NOVEL OF GLOBAL MYSTERY AND MURDER

iUniverse books may be ordered through booksellers or by contacting:

iUniverse
1663 Liberty Drive
Bloomington, IN 47403
www.iuniverse.com
1-800-Authors (1-800-288-4677)

On the cover: Scenic view of Lucerne, Switzerland against the Alps background

ISBN: 978-1-4917-7746-6 (sc)
ISBN: 978-1-4917-7747-3 (e)

Library of Congress Control Number: 2015915090

Print information available on the last page.

iUniverse rev. date: 09/24/2015

For my amazing son Paul with my sincerest admiration.

Books By The Same Author

Non-Fiction Under The Name Thomas W. Becker

Pageant Of World Commemorative Coins, Whitman Publishing Company, Racine 1962.

The Coin Makers, Doubleday and Company, Garden City, 1969.

EISENHOWER The Man, The Dollar and The Stamps, The American Mint and Postal Society and Mintmaster Inc., 1971.

Exploring Tomorrow In Space, Sterling Publishing Company Inc., Garden City, 1972

Foreword by Dr. Wernher von Braun

Our American Coins. The U.S. Treasury Department, Bureau Of The Mint, Washington DC, 1972 (on contract).

Aerospace: Crossing The Space Frontier. University of Missouri, Center for Distance and Independent Study, Columbia, Mo. 1988, rev 1998. Gifted high school self-study course in the history of space technology 1920-present. Mid-term and Final exams.

Studying Planet Earth: The Satellite Connection. University of Missouri, Center for Distance and Independent Study, Columbia, Mo. 1997. Gifted high school self-study course in remote sensing and Earth studies. Mid-term and Final exams.

Eight Against The World: Warriors Of The Scientific Revolution. Author House Publisher, Bloomington, Indiana 2007.

A Season Of Madness: Life And Death In The 1960s. Author House Publisher, Bloomington, Indiana 2007.

The Race For Technology: Conquering The High Frontier. Author House Publisher, Bloomington, Indiana 2008.

Novels

A League Of Shadows. Xlibris Publishers, Bloomington, Indiana 2009.

The Cape May Protocol. Strategic Book Group, Durham, Connecticut, 2010.

The Road At St. Liseau. iUniverse, Bloomington, Indiana, 2015.

The Pilatus Enigma. iUniverse, Bloomington, Indiana, 2015

Cast of Characters

Locations: St. Louis, London, Edinburgh, Paris & Lyon (France), Amsterdam, Lucerne, Munich

Time Period: the present

Erika Stevens — lead female character, young attractive computer programmer who falls in love with detective Marc Stevens, becomes significant contributor to solving the mysteries of the gang of international thieves

Marc Edwards — lead male character, St. Louis/Manchester police Detective Lieutenant, falls in love with Erica, hired by Scotland Yard to help destroy an international gang of thieves

Ben Warner - St Louis (Manchester, Missouri) Police Chief

John Dobson — St. Louis FBI Special Agent In Charge, organizes law enforcement to destroy an international gang of thieves

Molly Rogers — Police Building Supervisor, St. Louis police department

Jeb Stone – Federal Marshal, Missouri Regional Marshals Office

Ian Brooks – Scotland Yard Chief Inspector, instrumental in bring gang of thieves to justice

Derek Childers - Assistant Scotland Yard Inspector, London

James Barker - Assistant Scotland Yard Inspector, London

Colonel Ted Richards - Commander of Ranger Company, U.S. 82nd Airborne Division

Colonel Walter Anderson – Commander, British 6th Airborne Division commandos

Bill Simmons – replaces Ian Brooks as Scotland Yard Chief Inspector, London

Mr. Lambert – sinister ringleader of an international gang of thieves and murderers

Contents

Contents

Author Preface

I'm continually asked where I get ideas for novels. I always tell people that, mostly, an author's creative ideas are based on life experiences and a good deal of armchair research. The following explanations for this novel are good examples.

The storyline of *The Pilatus Enigma*, including the characters, is completely fictional, yet much of it is based on historical fact. The book's characters are fictional, but they represent bits and pieces of many different people. Research for the story was accomplished primarily from 1985 to 1994 while teaching space technology to Sixth Form students of the British National Space School in West London. Availing myself of many opportunities to travel throughout Europe, it was an unforgettable time when also I took copious amounts of photographs to use later in my teaching career in America and elsewhere. At that time, I had no idea I would end up as a writer.

The idea for *The Pilatus Enigma* novel developed in 2014 when I was retired and searching my mind for a good story. You might say, then, that this story took thirty years suddenly to come together in my head on a warm spring day when I had time to reflect on a whole host of life experiences. The story just "popped" into my creative thinking. Luckily, I kept all the photographs from those thirty years. Those memories of people and places of thirty years ago are still fresh in my mind.

Scotland Yard's headquarters are real, as are the Pilatus location, Trafalgar Square and the Sherlock Holmes Restaurant where I enjoyed some delightful dinners. Many scenes surrounding Lucerne, Switzerland and the trek up Mount Pilatus are indelibly stamped into my memory. All the other locations alluded to in the story are historically accurate as well. I was privileged to visit all the places mentioned in this book, sometimes more than once.

My Welsh friend Jim Potter, one of the co-teachers back in those days and a working geologist, continually bragged to me about Tenby, Wales, where some of his family members live. As a result, I often teased him about the town until he broke down and invited me there for several days. That visit turned out to be one of the most memorable experiences of my lifetime, resulting in several hundred photographs I keep in my files. He doesn't yet know I made Tenby a major location in the novel. Won't he be surprised!

My original purpose for attending university was to pursue degrees in clinical psychology. After graduation, I went back for another year to obtain a degree with a certificate in secondary education. The course of study I followed heavily emphasized abnormal human behavior, especially psychopathic and sociopathic illness. I studied many bizarre cases. Pieces from many of them emerge as the strange character *Gustav Blaatner* in this novel. Many of those cases made me shiver. I also did two summers intern work in a state mental institution for close-up studies of schizophrenia and manic-depressive (bipolar) psychosis. Some of those experiences, too, are touched on in this novel.

For forty-five years or so, I constantly carried a camera on my lap everywhere I went. My friends began to think I had some kind of obsessive-compulsive problem; other people thought I was just a tourist. During those days, I knew that when I retired someday

I most likely would want to write about some of my experiences and would need photographs to go with the writings. By the time I actually retired it became obvious I had photographed America and Europe during a half-century of history. Today, I continually rely on those pictures to give public presentations and illustrate written works.

In addition, I'm very visually oriented; I see the world around me in terms of pictures and images - in color. I still frequently carry a camera, and I love to photograph sunrises and sunsets, especially when they involve large bodies of water.

Living in a foreign country is essential to understand how a foreign culture operates on a daily basis. It's impossible to know Lucerne unless your feet have walked over it visiting shops, restaurants, and just getting from one place to another. If the city is mentioned in this book, my feet were there.

Since I was immersed in space technology during most of my career, there were times when it was necessary to touch base with government agencies such as the Federal Bureau of Investigation, Central Intelligence Agency, National Aeronautics and Space Administration, National Oceanic and Atmospheric Administration, and others in America. Beyond America's borders, I enjoyed relationships with the European Space Agency and the governments of Canada, Australia, India, China, Japan and the former Soviet Union. Associating with these agencies provided occasional creative chances to draw experiences for the novel. I wish to thank them for their support and advice over the years.

If you are interested in Europe, you might enjoy another novel about espionage, adventure and romance titled *The Road at St. Liseau* (2015), also published by iUniverse. The setting for that book takes place entirely in Europe.

The storyline in the present book begins briefly in St. Louis and quickly swings to Europe, developing as a race to find and arrest a gang of international thieves and murderers. The novel is a proverbial mixture of fact and fiction. Sometimes it is difficult to determine where one begins and the other leaves off.

I'm indebted to the publisher for excellent production of the book; especially the Design Team that made the book come alive in words and pictures. Throughout the overall production, the kind of informed, professional comment I received constantly helped develop the storyline along the way.

I hope you enjoy reading *The Pilatus Enigma* as much as I enjoyed writing it.

Prologue

After six long years of bloodshed and sacrifice, World War II in Europe came to an end on May 8, 1945 at a little schoolhouse in Rheims, Germany. The documents of German surrender were signed on an unlikely little table without either fanfare or anger, and there remained only the defeat of Japan to seal the record on the most costly and grievous conflict in the annals of human history.

The Allied Military Tribunal, established to call to account the designers of six years of Nazi immoral and despicable degradation, was more popularly referred to as The Nuremberg Trials (International Military Tribunal). The trials began six months after the surrender of Germany and lasted a year.

Those in the highest echelons of Adolph Hitler's Third Reich were charged with the darkest of war crimes against humanity; torture, slavery, instant death, concentration camps and other equally unimaginable acts of terror and brutal behavior, were brought to trial in the Tribunal courtrooms. Sentences ranging from years of imprisonment to death by hanging were imposed upon the criminals responsible for such an inhuman culture. Hitler and his mistress Eva Braun committed suicide; Joseph Goebels, wife and children, committed suicide. Herman Goering committed suicide in his jail cell before his death sentence could be carried out.

One doctor in particular, Dr. Rudolph Blaatner, Director of Medicine at Auschwitz concentration camp, was found guilty of extermination policies, human experimentation, female slavery policy, crimes against humanity, and aeromedical experiments. He was sentenced to death by hanging. It was rumored at the time that Blaatner's life partner, Gertrude, whom the doctor never married, gave birth to a baby boy known as Gustav, a few years before Dr. Blaatner was executed. Also it was rumored Gertrude committed suicide shortly after the execution. No record was ever found of the young boy's whereabouts after that date, and no record exists of his early childhood until his graduation from lower school.

Gustav Blaatner, now seventeen years old, turned the knob on the door to the Headmaster's office and calmly went in. Not knowing why he was asked to report to the office, he simply took a seat on one of the available stiff-backed chairs and waited. For seventeen long years, Gustav foraged for his survival, managing to stay alive by his own wiles. He never forgave his mother and father for abandoning him at such a young age. Occasionally, his refusal to grant them forgiveness showed up in unusually angry behavior aimed at the culture he barely understood. He always managed to keep from being put in prison, but his activities during spells of psychological imbalance often pushed him into a warped view of the life he was forced to embrace.

Gustav kept to himself at school most of the time. Because of his superior intellect, he found it difficult at times to interact with fellow students. His job at the grocery store kept him busy after school and prevented him from socializing with classmates, especially girls his own age. It was difficult, too, for Gustav to trust others and this trust issue frequently showed up in his interactions with the opposite sex.

"You can go in, now, he's expecting you," the office secretary addressed him. Gustav rose and went through the inner door.

"Gustav, lad, it's good to see you," the Headmaster greeted him. "Sit down and we'll talk a while, I have some good news for you."

"Thank you, sir," the young boy replied.

"There's someone I want you to meet, he'll be here in a moment," the Headmaster said. "I've been looking over your record. It's quite an impressive record of achievement. You're graduating this year after only three years of upper class instead of the usual four years. You're the first boy ever to achieve this outstanding accomplishment in our school's history. You should be quite proud of yourself."

"I suppose so," Gustav said meekly.

"What are your plans now that you're ready for bigger and better things?" the older man asked.

"I don't have any plans, sir. I guess I'll keep working in the grocery store until something shows up. I have to earn my room and board."

The Headmaster's door opened and a much older man strolled in. Gustav took note of the man's white beard and moustache, and judged him to be in his seventies or eighties. The man walked with a slight limp, carrying with him a cane which he occasionally used to tap on the floor.

"Hello, Heinrich, good to see you," the Headmaster offered. The two men shook hands and then the bearded man turned toward Gustav.

"So this is our young genius, is it?"

"Of course, meet Gustav Blaatner, winner of this year's Honors Award in science and mathematics. He has quite a record."

"Science AND mathematics — in only three years! You must have worked quite hard to achieve all that."

Gustav sat upright. "It was fun," the young boy smiled, "I'd like to learn more."

"And so you shall," Heinrich grinned. "How would you like to attend the Berlin Medical Institute and study medicine and physics? That should certainly keep you busy for a while."

"I don't have the money to pay for that," Gustav lamented.

"Well, now, I have a proposition for you," Heinrich sat down and leaned forward. "Doctors at the Institute are looking for promising young men who can master the medical curriculum and become a doctor of medicine. Think you can do that?"

"I've never thought about becoming a doctor," Gustav scratched his head.

"You'll have to give up your work at the grocery store so you can concentrate on your studies," Heinrich told him. "The Institute will pay all your expenses - everything, including a small amount of living money. In exchange you'll have to give up two years of your life after you're a doctor to teach at the Institute for those two years. After that, we'll help set you up in your own private practice, but you'll need to make yourself available to do some consulting work for the Institute. How does all that sound?"

"It's all too wonderful, I can't believe it," Gustav suddenly came alive. "When does all this begin?"

"About a month after you receive your graduation certificate from this lower school, say in early October."

"I'll be ready," Gustav sounded excited.

"We'll send you a letter of invitation in a week or so and get you enrolled. It's a simple matter."

"How can I ever thank you?" Gustav beamed.

"Well, you really can't," Heinrich smiled, "just prove we made the right decision by choosing you – work hard." The Headmaster patted Gustav's shoulder. "You'll be set for life," he smiled again, "you'll do fine, just work hard. Are you coming to the graduation dance next week?"

"I don't know how to dance, besides, I don't have a suit to wear."

"Don't worry about all that," the Headmaster countered, "some pretty young girl will teach you how to dance. It's easy, really."

Several days later, the school dance hall in the gymnasium featured tables, balloons and a six-piece band. Gustav was awed by the many students who dressed up and came to the affair. The Headmaster was right, he thought, it was a chance to meet other students, and especially girls. He never had time to socialize because of his work at the grocery store, but mainly because he spent every spare moment studying. Now, however, he marveled at the music and the girls in their frilly dresses, so he watched them dancing, wondering if he could learn the steps and the whirls around the dance floor. Gustav had never known a girl before now, but today for the first time he began to wonder about them.

"You're Gustav, aren't you," she ventured as she looked him over.

"How did you know that?" he smiled.

"Oh, everybody knows you," she giggled and flashed her eyelids. "They say you're a genius. Are you a genius?"

"No, I'm just a student. I wanted to be sure I'd graduate, so I studied a lot."

She looked up at him. "My name's Helga. Do you want to dance with me?"

"I don't know how to dance," he said shyly, "can you teach me?

"It's easy, c'mon to the dance floor," she encouraged him.

She showed him how to hold her and then how to move his feet in time to the slower kind of music. Gustav was surprised at how warm and soft she felt with his arm around her waist. He became enamored with how lightly she moved along the floor with him. They danced almost every dance as the evening went on, talking about this and that and getting to know each other.

After a while in the crowded gymnasium, her cheeks became flushed and she was breathing harder.

"Why don't we go outside," she suggested, "it's really warm in here." She took his hand and led him out the door into the cool evening.

"Do you want to kiss me?" she asked softly, tilting her head to one side.

He had never kissed a girl, not even touched one, but her femininity and her boldness began to arouse him so he leaned over and gave her a quick kiss on her lips.

"That was too short," she giggled again. "Do it longer, hold your breath or breathe through your nose, and put your arms around my waist again. That's it."

They kissed several times and he felt something stirring inside him. She took one of his hands and placed it on her breast. Gustav began to tingle.

"You can touch me anywhere you want to, it feels good, don't be shy. I won't hurt you," she giggled again.

He slid his hands down over her buttocks and massaged them. When she reached between his legs and squeezed him, he felt himself taken over by feelings he had never had before and he kissed her at the same time, over and over again. Helga led him across the spacious grass quadrangle into a secluded woods away from the gymnasium, then turned and looked at him. "Put your hand up my dress," she urged him.

At her insistence, he slid his hand up the softness of her thighs and explored the region between her legs. After a few moments, they found themselves on the ground and she taught him about the delights of her body. For Gustav, it was all a miracle too wonderful as they moved to the urging of their bodies. He looked down at her pretty face and red lips, and suddenly became a man far beyond his years of adolescence. His future was assured, at least for the next six years, and now he had made love to a pretty young girl.

During his first year of medical school, less than a year later, they were seeing each other often. He studied constantly learning about the structure of the human body and examining the many parts of human anatomy. The young girl Helga was found murdered in her apartment and her body mutilated. The police never solved the case and it still is a mystery to this day.

1

Summertime came to Missouri, calling forth the beauty of flowers and the richness of the farm belt. It was a bright Saturday morning without a cloud in the sky, a typical St. Louis summer morning. Erika Stevens stood in the middle of her living room, still with a kitchen towel in her hands, staring at first one wall and then another. Something was wrong. It all just didn't look right. She thought maybe if she changed her position, everything would look better from a different perspective, so she began moving from place to place around the living room.

Maybe if she moved some pieces of furniture. . .no, it didn't work. . .it all still looked wrong, there still was too much empty space on the walls. Perhaps her job as a computer programmer had jaded her creativity. Too much digital data all week long might be blocking her creative abilities. Then all of a sudden a single idea struck her. That was it – there was too much empty space. She needed another piece of artwork to fill that emptiness. All she had to do was move the pictures on the wall around a bit and make the empty space a little larger. Having done that, the bigger space was just made for another painting.

The promising excitement of a new adventure was just what she needed, she thought, something to shake her out of the drab existence of eight hours a day pounding on a computer keyboard. She was an excellent computer programmer working for a highly respected company. A college degree had fine-tuned her skills to a sharp edge and the challenging assignments that came her way kept her on top of every new type of digital development. Still, there was something undeniably missing in her life. She always felt a little on the lonely side no matter what she was doing or wherever she happened to be. Whatever it was, it left a nagging empty place in her psyche she couldn't seem to fill. Perhaps she was just lonely after all, and wouldn't admit it to herself.

Erika was a comely young woman who made a point of always looking neat and tidy. At age thirty, she was attractive with a trim figure. Her brunette hair surrounding a well-kept face with full lips and dark brown eyes usually caused men to look at her more than once. She followed her physical exercises at the gym several times a week to fight off the threat of spreading hips, yet the men she met there seemed more boyish rather than mature. In spite of her striking appearance, she never was able to find a man who she felt had something promising to offer.

Grabbing a light jacket and scarf in spite of the warm sunshine, she retreated out the door and headed for Susan's Art Shop, operated by one of the more successful one-owner businesses in suburban St. Louis. Grimacing from the brightness of an early morning sun, she set out on the *great Saturday adventure*. Breezing through the door of the art shop, she was greeted by her life-long friend. Susan would know exactly what to do. Susan always had lots of good ideas and over the years had made more of an impact on her own life than she realized. She and Susan first met at the beginning of high school and they became close friends through thick and thin, even at college.

"Erika!" Susan wailed across the room, "I haven't seen you for several months. Where have you been keeping yourself?"

"I've been in hiding waiting for Mr. Right," Erika laughed as the two gave each other a hug. "Actually," Erika continued, "I've been working undercover for the *Man Patrol* but I haven't hit pay dirt yet. I don't have very many suspects but I keep looking. And you're busy as usual, I see."

"Yes, just got in a consignment of new paintings," Susan countered with a sigh. "Work, work, work – there's no end to it."

"That's what you get for being such a successful entrepreneur, which really is why I'm here today. I need your expert opinion. There's a big gap on my living room wall and I need to find an exceptional piece of art to fill it."

Susan put down her clipboard and looked across at Erika for a few seconds. "Still looking for Mr. Right, are you? How are you getting along with. . .Kevin, I think you said his name is?" Erika gave a short sigh of frustration.

"Oh. . .he's okay for a movie date, I suppose, or an evening at the symphony, but I've seen better movies on TV. . .he's just not THE ONE. He hasn't even tried to ravish me yet. I'm sadly disappointed."

Susan walked over and stood face to face with her long-time friend.

"Erika, what are we going to do with you," the storeowner chided her. "Here you are only thirty years old, VERY attractive with a fabulous, enviable body, a lot of fun and working at a successful job. Don't you think, maybe, our requirements are just a bit too high? I mean, I bet your Sir Gallahad, whoever he turns out to be, doesn't even ride a white horse, does he?"

Ignoring Susan's question, Erika began looking around the shop, finally turning back toward Susan.

"It's better to go through a whole bunch of rejects rather than spend my life with the wrong man. None of the men I meet ever seem to have any substance to them. They're just little boys floating along without any real direction. It gets to be frustrating at times."

Susan wheeled around and faced her again. "Peck...peck...peck," she said, "you're like a hen in a barnyard – picky, picky, picky - I bet you haven't even been laid yet, have you? Meanwhile, life moves on – a wrinkle here, a mole there, and suddenly you're over the hill with nothing but memories of a lot of worse-than-normal bad dates. You're my best friend, Erika, and a helluva good catch. I love you like a sister and I hate to see you join the what's-her-name club."

"Oh . . .look at that one," Erika suddenly exclaimed, pointing to one of the paintings on the counter. "That's beautiful, don't you think . . .moody, like you could lose yourself in the perspective? I'd like to climb that mountain. I like it!"

She held the painting up, turning it this way and that to catch the light on it at just the right angle. "It kind of has a challenge to it, like there are other worlds out there, new challenges to meet and new horizons to cross. I really like it," Erika squealed.

"Yes, but it doesn't have much character to it," Susan pointed out. "It's just a mountain, a pile of rocks like your man-hunting strategy. Anyone can paint that kind of art, even a beginner. In spite of your attachment to it, it really doesn't have any depth to it. It's static – just sits there and looks back at you. How about this one – very *avant garde*," Susan pointed out, holding a painting at arm's length. "How big a painting do you want it to be?"

"No, no. . .I want this one," Erika swooned, "it suits my mood today. I want to climb that mountain, get to the top and lose myself in what's on the other side."

"You sound like you're searching for the meaning of life – *your life* – and you haven't found it yet. How about this one?"

Erika frowned. "Too modern, it looks like an eye test, and there isn't any feeling in it. I could paint that one with a ruler and a compass. No, I like this one. How much is it?" she asked, juggling the painting.

"The artist thinks it's one step below the Mona Lisa," Susan laughed. "The rest of us call it Mount Ranier, but for you, my dear, I'll give it away at twenty-five dollars – and it's about an eleven-by-seventeen, that ought to plug your hole – I mean the one on the wall." They both laughed.

"I'll take it," Erika said wistfully, "maybe it will perk me up. Wrap it up to go, I'm anxious to see how it looks on the wall. Maybe it will give me a new incentive."

"Sure you don't want to look around a little?" Susan queried.

"No, no, I liked it the minute I set eyes on it," Erika sounded excited by new prospects.

Erika eagerly watched Susan carefully wrapping her new prized possession. Handing her the package, Susan reached out and touched her arm.

"I'm not trying to mother you, hon, it's just that I worry about you. You deserve much more in life if you'd just let yourself go and live a little. I'll tell you what, if you come over for dinner soon, Fred and I promise not to pick on you. Give me a call." With a wave of her hand, Erika disappeared out the door, promising to get in touch.

Mount Ranier, Washington State

Midweek the following week, she stood before her new acquisition with growing admiration, eventually moving about the room to view it from a variety of different points. Her brow furrowed. It was then that she discovered something odd about the painting. Near the middle of the scene, it looked as if a piece of the artwork was starting to flake off. She immediately rushed up and took the painting down, laying it flat on the living room sofa, bending over it for a closer look.

Yes, undeniably, a small section of the painting, perhaps a little more than an inch or so square, was starting to curl up slightly near the center of the scene. With her fingernail, she tried to lift the errant piece of canvas. Devastated and frustrated, she put the painting in a shopping bag and headed back to the store. *That's what comes of buying a cheap piece of work. The old adage was right, "You get what you pay for" still held true,* she thought. This would never do, she decided, her newest piece of art was already coming apart and she had it only four days.

Rushing through the front door of Susan's Art shop, Erika squealed for Susan. "Sue," she shouted, "there's something wrong with. . ."

She never finished the sentence when she realized the store was a complete shambles. Paintings, frames, papers and various kinds of little pieces of artwork littered the floor as if a whirlwind had swept through the usually well-kept premises. None of the sculptures was broken or moved. Various paintings and frames were strewn about in total disarray.

Marching toward the cash register, she stepped closer through the piles of paintings and found Susan's body in a pool of blood on the floor behind the counter. In total shock, she screamed as loud as she could while little ribbons of tears flowed down her cheeks. She shrank back in horror and covered her mouth. Almost automatically, she fumbled through her purse for her cell phone and dialed 9-1-1. Susan's eyes were still open, staring widely at nothing. Erika choked several times, finding it difficult to breathe.

By now she was close to being hysterical and she thought she was going to vomit. Who could have done this to her best friend?

"9-1-1 – what is your emergency?" a voice answered. Trembling and choking back the tears, she managed to reply to the operator. "My friend, Susan . . .she's been killed, she's dead. . .and her store is a mess, everything's topsy-turvy. Help, help. . ." Susan's body was in an awkward position, her skirt pushed up her thighs and her blouse almost torn to shreds. She looked as if she had put up a struggle.

"Give me your name and location please, and stay on the line, don't hang up," the voice directed.

"I. . .I can't stand up," Erika stammered between sobs, "she's dead, someone killed her."

Carefully, the operator tried to calm her down. "DON'T TOUCH ANYTHING, give me your name and address, please."

"My name is Erika Stevens, I'm at Susan's Art Store, on Manchester Road, and she's dead. Please help me."

Erika barely heard the emergency operator. Looking around again, she noticed the cash register drawer standing open as well as the file cabinet just below the drawer. Papers and file jackets were strewn all over the floor; receipts, inventory files, pictures and odd pieces of notepaper littered the entire area. Erika leaned against the counter to steady herself. She felt nauseous and lightheaded and stumbled over her own feet.

"Stay there, the police are already on the way, don't hang up, you'll need to talk to the police. Can you hear me?"

"Yes. . .yes. . .hurry, my best friend," Erika continued sobbing and choking back an avalanche of tears. "What's happened, why did this happen?" she questioned herself. Looking over at Susan's body in such an awkward position, she wondered if her friend had been molested. Her pants were still in the right place, but her body had dark bruises all over it, especially on her face and shoulders. Erika knew in an instant that Susan had been beaten very thoroughly. Erika turned away from the gruesome scene and began sobbing again.

She began to hear police sirens in the distance. Out of the corner of her eye, she saw through the front window of the store two rough-looking men running across the street toward her. She wondered if they were the cause of the tragedy. Outside on the other side of the street, she had only the briefest glimpse of a man starting to run toward the store between the parked cars. Bald-headed, he wore a short brown leather jacket and pressed his face right up to the front window.

Still clutching her painting and fighting back the onrushing tears, she moved across the room trying to look as inconspicuous as possible. There was no place to hide and the two men were coming through the doorway carrying guns in their hands. The third man, trying to see inside the store, put his face between his hands up to the window as if to shade his eyes.

The other two ruffians burst through the front entrance, smashing the glass door and frame. "What do you have in the package?" one of the men shouted, "give me the package!" Immediately one of the men fired several shots at her as she knelt down behind the counter. "I'll get you, you know that," one of the men called out, "so you might as well give me the package."

An arriving police car screeched to a stop in front of the store. Two officers came rushing through the broken door with guns drawn. An immediate firefight broke out between the police and the two unknown men. Bullets were flying everywhere as Erika lay flat behind the counter trying to shield herself from the bullets.

"This is badge 41729 at 963 Manchester Road, request back up, shots fired, armed robbery in progress," one of the officers shouted into his shoulder radio.

Bullets whizzed above her head and she cut her knee from the broken glass on the floor as she lay flat trying to hide from her assailants.

"Stay calm," the 9-1-1 operator continued as bullets sped through the air. "Have the police arrived yet? Are they there now?"

"Yes, yes," Erika whispered, "they're shooting at me and at each other."

"If you can hide, stay concealed and keep quiet," the operator went on. "More police are on the way. What do you think happened there?" Erika began to shake when a bullet slammed into the counter directly in front of her. "I don't know, I can't tell. I just want out of here before I get killed!"

"Stay where you are, keep as calm as you can, and don't move," the operator repeated.

The firefight stopped as suddenly as it began. Peering carefully over the top of the counter, Erika could see the two officers were unhurt but there was no sign of the two hoodlums. The police holstered their guns. One of them called out loud.

"Is anyone here? This is the police, come out with your hands over your head. We won't harm you if you do as we say. Come out now," the officer's voice was calm and steady. He thought he heard sounds coming from behind the counter and came closer, approaching cautiously. Still clutching the painting, Erika stood up and held the painting high over her head. "Where are those men? They tried to kill me!" she stammered, half-frightened and half-furious with anger.

Jefferson National Expansion Memorial Arch, St. Louis

"They're over here on the floor, probably dead by now," one of the policemen replied. Scrutinizing her cautiously, he figured she might be a customer. "You're not in any danger now," he said. "How did you get mixed up in this, anyway? What happened here? What's your name, how long have you been here?"

"I came here to talk to Susan, the store owner, about this painting. She and I have been close friends for twenty years. I found her on the floor dead, and then those horrible men came running in the door shooting at me." The tears flowed down her face despite her attempt to hold them back. For a moment once more, she thought she was going to throw up and reached out to the edge of the counter to steady herself.

"One of the detectives just got here," the officer said, "I'm sure he'll want to talk to you, you're the only witness we have. Come over here and sit down, he'll be with you in a minute. Can I get you something, a glass of water maybe?" Erika slowly shook her head no.

The store began to overflow with uniformed policemen, some of them taking pictures and others rummaging through the debris. Erika sat quietly in a nearby chair trying to regain her composure when she saw another pedestrian peering through the window at her. She shifted in her chair uncomfortably and stared back at him. An officer reached out to her to show his badge and credentials.

"Hello, I'm detective Marc Edwards from the Manchester–St. Louis PD, and you are. . .?"

"I'm Erika Stevens, Susan was my best friend, I can't believe all this is happening," she said. Erika wrung her hands. The tears started again and she tried to control herself, fumbling with a damp handkerchief that by now was soaked with tears from her grief and the ordeal she witnessed.

"Are you up to just a few questions?" Edwards ventured. "I won't keep you long, but eventually I'd like you to come to the police station for some more lengthy conversation. What time did you arrive here, Miss Stevens, approximately?"

"About one-thirty, I guess, I'm not really sure," Erika sniffled. "I don't even know what time it is right now."

"What did you see when you first came into the store?" Marc asked.

"Well. . .everything was a mess. . .paintings and papers strewn all over the floor. It was highly unlike Susan, she was always very neat and organized. It looks almost as if someone ransacked the place. I knew right away something was wrong, then I saw her lying there in the middle of all that blood." Erika slowly looked up at the detective. "She's dead, isn't she?"

"I'm afraid so," Edwards replied as sensitively as he could. "When did the men come into the store? I mean, how long were you here before they came in?"

"Oh. . . just a minute or so. They ran in so fast and started shouting at me, then they shot at me several times and demanded I give up the painting, so I ducked behind the counter . . .the bullets went over my head."

"They wanted the painting that fast? That's the first thing they said to you?"

"Yes, they didn't care about me, all they were interested in was the painting, a picture of Mount Ranier I think."

"Where's the painting now?" Edwards pressed onward.

"Right here beside me, on the floor. I'm afraid I got blood on it, I cut my knee on some broken glass." Erika reached down and retrieved the shopping bag, handing it over to the detective.

"Do you know either of the men who came in right behind you?" the Detective asked.

"No, never saw them before, but they were holding guns when they came through the door."

"Did you ever see either of the men here in the store when you came to see Susan?" Edwards asked

"No, no," Erika answered a little gruffly, a signal to the detective she was getting aggravated at the constant barrage of questions. Edwards picked up the shopping bag and slid the painting out. After looking at it a moment, he noticed a strip of the scene was coming loose.

"Was the painting damaged like this when you first arrived?"

"I guess so, I bought it three days ago, but when I saw it was coming apart I brought it back. That's the reason I returned it,

13

because it was damaged," Erika explained quietly with outstretched arms.

The detective looked over at her as he took a business card from his shirt pocket. "Here's my card, Miss Stevens, with my telephone number and address on it. I'm going to take the painting with me, but I'd like for you to come down to the station, say, in about two days, where we can have a quiet conversation. Will you do that? We'll send a police car for you if you'll call us when you're ready to come down."

"Yes, I guess so. I'd like to go home now, if you don't mind."

"Of course, you must be very tired from this nightmare. If you think of something in the meantime, don't hesitate to call. The telephone is right on my desk."

"Gary, will you take this young lady home?" he asked, turning toward one of the officers. "Walk her up to her front door, she doesn't look too steady on her feet."

The officer nodded, then turning aside, he spoke softly to Marc. "The medical examiner says the victim's been dead about two hours."

Marc nodded in agreement. He studied Erika as she got up to leave, not just to make certain she was steady enough on her feet, but to watch her movements as well. Young, very pretty and obviously in shock, she kept her composure and answered him question for question. She was the only witness to what might have happened, but at the moment she was too shaken up to answer detailed questions.

"Is there someone at home, a parent or sister, or maybe your husband?" Marc called after her. It was a very important question for Marc, requiring a very important answer and he wasn't going to miss the opportunity to find out if she was single. Erika turned toward him slightly.

"No. . .there's no one, I take care of myself. I'm not married, I live alone." Marc was relieved when she said she wasn't married, and he began to take a renewed interest in her.

Marc stayed a few minutes after she left, then climbed into his unmarked patrol car and headed for the police station carrying the painting on the back seat. After several moments of looking into his rear view mirrors, he began to suspect the car behind him was tailing him.

"Central Station, this is Car 19," Marc spoke into his radiophone, "request an unmarked car meet me at the corner of Sixth and Chestnut as soon as possible. Code 3, be aware of a possible tail car behind me."

On Thursday, Erika sat demurely in front of the detective's desk at police headquarters. The room was filled with people, police and civilians coming and going noisily as usual. She stared at the floor in silence, waiting for the detective to return to his desk when he arrived in a flurry.

"Sorry to keep you waiting," Marc apologized, "we're having a heavy day. Here, let me take your jacket."

"No, I'm okay now," Erika spoke up, "what is it you wanted to see me about?"

Marc leaned against the desk momentarily, gathering his thoughts together.

"I wanted to give you time to recover from the shock of seeing your friend dead. We've worked through the weekend on this case and we keep coming back to the same conclusion. Everything keeps coming back to the painting, so we have a theory we'd like to explain to you and see what you think. Ready?" Erika nodded. Marc offered one more piece to the story.

"The two men who shot at you are known criminals with long rap sheets. The painting came from a new consignment the owner hadn't been able to inventory yet. The shooters couldn't find a record of your name as the buyer because you paid cash. There was no credit card, no written check, so there is no record of you as a buyer which means they figured you would come back to the store when you found something wrong with the painting. They decided to stake out the store, hoping you would turn up. Now, here's question number one.

When you first reached the front door of the Art Store, several things happened all at once," Marc began. "Look here at this chain of events written on the chalkboard. First, you entered carrying the painting. Second, the two men got out of their car and started across the street. Third, someone got out of a second car across the street, looked through the front window, and then stopped to wait and see what was happening. Fourth, several shots were fired, then more shots, and you screamed. Are you still with me, Miss Stevens?" Erika nodded politely.

Marc stood up straight. "All these events happened at the same time, barely minutes apart. It's obvious the key to their relationship with each other is the painting. The ransacked store, the death of your friend, your refusal to give up the painting, the men shooting at you, are all tied together. What's so important about the painting?"

"Nothing, it's just a painting of a mountain," Erika repeated. "It's supposed to be Mount Ranier, I think, but I'm not certain of that."

Marc sat down again behind his desk. "We need to be a little less formal. Call me Marc and I'll call you Erika, is that ok?"

"Fine," Erika said.

"Now, let's get back to the painting," Marc began again. "We examined the painting carefully, in fact we sent it downtown to the crime lab and guess what, they made an important discovery.

On the back of the little piece of canvas that was coming loose, they found a small, square piece of metal. When they removed the disc, they discovered a message on it. They couldn't decipher the message so we sent the painting - and the disc - to the FBI laboratory at Quantico, Virginia. We should hear back from them by the end of the week. But I have a few more questions to ask you, is that ok?" Erika nodded she understood.

"Do you remember seeing anyone else in the street besides the two men who shot at you?" She thought for a moment then shook her head no.

Marc noted that, in her testimony a few days ago, Erika said there was a third man who crossed the street and looked through the front window of the art shop. Putting this inconsistency aside for the moment, he decided just to continue his questions.

"How well do you know the store owner?"

"I've known her all my adult life," Erika replied. "Why is that important?"

"To your knowledge, has she ever been involved in anything illegal?" Marc continued.

"No – never. She isn't that kind of person, she's straight as an arrow, has a husband and a baby girl about five years old."

Marc picked up the conversation. "When I left the crime scene, I saw someone following me in another car. When I investigated, I learned he was driving a stolen car, but he managed to elude the police car tagging along behind me; so now we're back to the painting again. It's the *single most important piece of evidence* in this entire puzzle; we put it through every test we possibly could, but found nothing else unusual. Why did you choose this particular painting?"

"I like the scene because it's moody, you can sort of lose yourself in it," Erika confided. "It has great perspective and because the mountain is so obvious, yet it doesn't detract from the whole scene.

I loved it – now I'm not sure I'll ever get it back – in fact I'm not sure I want to get it back, it reminds me of this whole tragedy."

"Yes you will, I'll see that you get it back. One more question. Will you let me take you to dinner tonight since I've been beating on you for three days now?"

"Yes, I'd like that," Erika perked up at the invitation, "if I can choose the restaurant."

Reflecting on the detective's invitation, she wondered why she accepted a dinner date from a man she didn't know, and she began to see the detective in a different way now. She wondered about all the usual questions she wished she could ask him out loud. He was nice looking in a rugged sort of way, and he was very careful and considerate of how he treated her with his questions. She also wondered if he was as much interested in her as the answers to the questions.

"That's a deal – just say where," he said.

"Georgio's." she smiled. "I love their chicken alfredo."

"One more thing before we leave," Marc paused. "There's a lot of *reckless desperation* running throughout this whole scenario. Ransacking the art store, killing the owner, bursting through the front door, shooting at you, threatening you, someone following me back to police headquarters – *uncontrolled desperation*. Why, why was everything so careless, so needless, really? That's an important question that has to be answered. These men could almost care less whether or not they get caught, anything – *anything* - as long as they got their hands on that painting. Why?"

Erika lifted her eyes and looked at Marc. He was a good-looking man, probably in his early thirties. His tousled brown hair nearly falling over his forehead accentuated his eagerness to find the answers to dozens of questions. He was very intelligent, she realized, and he knew how to think. All of this seemed to emphasize his solid frame and the way he carried himself across the room. Erika found herself suddenly looking for little kinks in his Camelot armor-like presenting of himself, and just as suddenly she dismissed all that was going through her mind when she was brought back to reality.

"I don't know, I don't think like you do," she answered, "guess I'm still in a semi-state of shock. It's only been a couple of days since. . ." She left the sentence unfinished.

"Well, let's get away from this mystery for a while," he offered, with a sizeable but rather boyish grin. "It's off to Giorgio's and chicken alfredo."

At the restaurant, they were greeted by a smiling waiter who found a table for two toward the more softly lit back of the room.

"Hello, Lieutenant, it's always good to see one of St. Louis' 'finest.'" Marc slipped the waiter a twenty-dollar bill, unseen by Erika as they seated themselves.

"The wine list, Leonardo, let's start with a nice mellow bottle." Looking over at Erika, he asked, "You do have a little wine once in a while?" It seemed more a statement than a question. Erika nodded. "The young lady is going to order chicken Alfredo — come to think of it, so am I."

"Of course, Lieutenant, how about a nice smooth white wine, if I may. It will go nicely with chicken alfredo."

"You're the expert, my man, we'll leave the choice up to you while we catch up with the day's interesting events." Marc held the chair for her to sit down.

"You're pretty young to be a detective Lieutenant, Marc, how did you get to such a high rank so fast?"

"Education," came his quick response. "I have a master degree in criminology and also went to the FBI Academy's Crime and Forensics year-long course. I never talk about this and I really don't know why I'm telling you. Just put it down to good luck, I suppose. But let's not talk about me, I want to know all about you, what kind of work you do, what you like to do for fun, not your life history but just a few highlights."

Marc looked over at her almost nonchalantly, trying to hide his real interest in her. She was very attractive, no doubt about that, and he was stirred by her honesty and perhaps her apparent innocence. Throughout their conversation over dinner, they quickly reached a moment of "human chemistry" that drew them closer together. Soon they were laughing and exchanging little stories as the evening slipped away.

Marc looked at his watch. "Do you realize what time it is?" he said abruptly. "Look at your watch."

"Oh, wow, I need to get home," Erika sounded surprised. "I have a boring meeting at nine a.m. if I'm sober, and I need to get some sleep."

"I have someone waiting to drive you home and I've asked one of the officers to bring your car around right away. What a wonderful evening, I can't remember when I've had such an enjoyable – three hours," he remarked, looking at his watch again. "We definitely need to do this again, and soon."

"I agree, I had a nice time, also," she smiled at him.

"You'll be hearing from me, quite soon in fact. Right now, we're going to switch cars very fast. The other car is pulling up beside me – open your door and jump in the back seat of the other car and the officer will take you home. Remember, don't hesitate to call any hour of the day or night. Be careful."

He wanted so much to kiss her and put his arms around her, but at this point she was still a person of semi-interest. Marc found it hard to believe that somehow she could be mixed up in this intrigue. He liked her, yes, but it was more than that. She was intelligent and quick witted, soft spoken, and he felt he could get to like her much more, too, if he knew her better. But what if he was wrong about her? What if she was part of an elaborate scheme? Time would tell, and he sincerely hoped she was innocent. Guess his caution came from being a policeman, he thought to himself.

The following morning, Erika went through her morning routine preparing for work. Dressed at last and having washed the breakfast dishes, her instincts nagged her to go room by room checking the doors and windows. While she was opening the curtains covering one of the living room windows, the window glass quickly shattered into a hundred pieces splattering broken glass all over her. At the same time, she heard something whiz past her ear. She jumped backward as another bullet hit the windowsill and still a third shot very lightly grazed her forearm.

Panic seized her, causing her to freeze where she was standing. They were after her again, and they were bent on killing her. A dozen questions crossed her mind at the same time, all mixed together. She could barely breathe at first, then screaming at the top of her voice, she ducked and ran to her purse to retrieve Marc's business card.

"Marc, help me, someone's shooting at my apartment, three or four times," she shouted in wide-open panic. "Come help me, I'm going to get killed, they're shooting at me again."

"Erika, listen to me – listen to what I'm saying – do you hear me?" Marc raised his voice. "Stay away from the windows, I'm on my way. Go to the bathroom, close the door and lock it, and lie down in the bathtub. Don't make a sound. I happen to be close by and I'll be there in less than five minutes with some officers. We'll get you out. Now hang up and go! I'm not very far from your house."

She did as he instructed just as another bullet drilled its way through a second window and she heard the glass splinters skitter across the carpeted floor. By now she was hysterical again and began to sob as she heard her front door being smashed open.

"Erika, Erika!" Marc shouted, "stay there, I'm coming, unlock the bathroom door." She recognized Marc's voice, jumped out of the tub, threw open the door and they rushed into each other's arms.

"Marc, I'm so scared, what are we going to do?" the words came tumbling out.

"Are you ok? I brought a SWAT team with me, they're combing the neighborhood right now." At that moment, they heard a volley of shots out in the street and a voice came over Marc's shoulder radio.

"Code Red, Code Red, shots fired, two officers down, send backup and a bus, hurry."

Marc's head jerked up. "There's a firefight out in the street below," Marc grimaced. "Two of my men have been shot and obviously there are at least two snipers, maybe more. Go back into the bathroom and scoot down in the tub again. I'll be right back."

"Full out desperation again," she heard Marc mumble as he ran off and out of the apartment. His radio crackled a second time.

"Marc, this is Chief Warner, get your victim back to the station, I'm surrounded by FBI men here and they don't look very happy. Make it quicker than quick."

"Right now, we're pinned down by some snipers," Marc answered nervously. "I have a SWAT team here – we'll be there as soon as it's safe to leave."

At the police station afterward, Marc and Erika went into the conference room and sat beside each other. She was still trembling from the morning's ordeal. Looking around, she noticed the room was filled with stern-looking men and women in suits and uniforms. At the podium, Manchester police Chief Ben Warner was the first to speak.

"I'm not going to introduce everyone, just take it for granted there are two federal Marshals, six FBI special agents and three PD uniforms in on this conference. Ladies and gentlemen, these are MPD Detective Lieutenant Marc Edwards, most of you know him already, and the very brave and attractive young lady is Erika Stevens, who still is the initial victim in this case. She's had a very bad morning, dodging bullets from her assailants. This is twice there were attempts to kill her. She was the first person to find the art store ransacked and its owner murdered. She wasn't in the store when the perps did their work, but she was the first person on the scene afterward.

I'm going to turn the podium over to FBI Special Agent In Charge John Dobson from the D.C. field office, who has some amazing things to say to all of us in spite of not having any sleep last night. Be prepared, this is going to get complicated. Also, you'll notice the television cameras around the room are operating."

Dobson began his presentation, looking at his audience with a solemn face."

"Quickly summarized," Dobson began, "you have all stumbled upon an international criminal and spy ring involving seven different nations all the way from the UK to Italy, and even South America. Other countries may be involved that we don't know about yet. By the way, this conference is being simultaneously broadcast to law enforcement in all the countries concerned.

Please don't be upset by my announcing that this case now becomes a federal jurisdiction case with the FBI as the point group, which in most instances makes it an extremely sensitive matter. We've named this international case *Operation Lady Luck* in honor of our key witness and continuous target here, Miss Stevens. Hopefully we'll all be able to finish what she started.

The code name for the case in America now becomes *Copper Canyon*. When you mention this code name, it will immediately get everyone's attention. The code name also carries explicit permission, all the way up to the White House including the Departments of Justice and Homeland Security, to be armed at all times and allowed extreme force – shoot first and ask questions later. This very well organized gang of international criminals will stop at nothing, as you already know. Wait a second or two longer, and we'll send flowers to your funeral. These aren't common criminals.

On the screen in front of you is an image of the painting Miss Stevens purchased at Susan's Art Shop. This next close-up image now shows a part of the painting that came loose and began to curl up. Evidently someone didn't glue it down very well. Marc sent the painting and the loose piece of canvas to the FBI lab where it was gone over very meticulously. That's when we found the next close-up image of a miniature data chip about an inch square. It carries a message in digital data. We've worked all week trying to decode the message and we were finally successful. Here it is:

BEGIN APRIL 1 GUNS FRANCE TO ITALY XX SEND COKE VENEZUELA TO DALLAS XX SHIP HEAVY ARMS NETHERLANDS TO COLOMBIA XX CAREFULLY WRAP PAINTINGS GOING TO SWITZERLAND XX INFORM MR LAMBERT AS USUAL XX

The first part of the message is obvious, but of course no one knows who Mr. Lambert is; we assume he's somewhere at the top of the criminal food chain."

Dobson signaled to turn off the television screen, took a short drink of water, and resumed his briefing

"Let's go back to Saturday. Miss Stevens bought the painting on Saturday. Tuesday she returned it to the store and that's where the story really begins. Two local hoods were killed trying to take the painting from her, after they tried to kill her. This morning, she again was the target of several snipers who tried to kill her as she was getting ready to leave for work. I think they fired some six or seven shots through her living room windows. We have some bullet casings and a few slugs from the walls. We have the perps in the morgue now and we also captured two of them. Unfortunately the dead can't talk and, even though they know they're facing murder charges, the two captured assassins won't give us any useful information.

Chief Warner says the hoods are well known in these parts so we can safely assume they were quick-hired for one job. They failed. This morning, Miss Stevens was the target for assassination again. It also failed, but as we speak several agents, I understand, have determined where they were shooting from and I think we recovered shell casings. The killers used sniper rifles. We'll know more in a few minutes."

"This case is so large we'll have to break into committees pretty soon," Dobson directed. "First committee will be Chief Warner, myself, Marc, Miss Stevens, and Building Supervisor Molly Rogers. You haven't met her yet, she's in charge of Protective Custody here at the station and she wears a weapon.

Miss Stevens, I'm afraid it's necessary, at Marc's request, to put you in protective custody until we can sort out all of this. It's an annoyance, I'm sure, but the only alternative is to turn you loose at the mercy of local hoods. Believe me, they WILL try to go at you again. You obviously saw something they're worried about, but we can't yet determine what that is."

A messenger came into the briefing with news the snipers are local hoods again. Dobson continued his briefing.

"Evidently the chief organizer is out-sourcing his local help. The next time the hoods attack, it will be a very carefully planned, split-second hit so. . .Marc and Erika, be on your toes. Stay out of the public view if you can."

Turning to a tall man behind him, the FBI agent held out his hand.

"This is Jeb Stone from the Marshals office, Erika, he has an alternative solution for you for the present time."

"Just something for you to think about," Stone began, reaching the podium. "If the hoods keep trying to get at you, Miss Stevens, we can offer asylum for you somewhere else in America, or even abroad if that's what you decide upon. The program I'm referring to is known as the Witness Protection Program.

You'll have to disappear — completely. No one must know where you are except the Marshal's office. We'll move all your belongings and furniture, give you a totally new name with driver's license, ID card with picture, Social Security card, credit cards, and bank account with your current balance. We'll even find a job for you at your present salary, but maybe not doing quite the same kind of work.

If you decide to go on the Program, you can NEVER come back to St. Louis, NEVER tell your relatives where you are. You'll even have to suddenly break off with your boyfriend if you have one. It's as if you just died without a funeral service. We probably will ask you to change your hair, make it a different color and style. You'll all of a sudden be born at thirty years old with no record of your childhood or education attainments. You'll have to make new friends and you can't tell anyone about your past life.

Incidentally, Miss Stevens, I've talked to Mr. John Foreman, your current boss, and briefly explained the situation. He said to tell you he's greatly disappointed, you're one of his best employees. Living a decent life does have its perks, right?"

Erika spoke up abruptly. "Wait, this is too much to think about right now. Do you need to have an answer right away? On the face of it, I don't like it. I'm enjoying my present life, I don't know if I want to give it up."

"That's entirely up to you, Miss Stevens," Stone went on, "but I need to caution you about something. You'll likely spend the rest of your life looking over your shoulder, even get shot at again, maybe numerous times. Whoever's the head of this ring of criminals is exceedingly intelligent. He can hire anyone he needs to stay on your trail, and even watch you taking a shower. If you get abducted, you'll die a terrible death, most likely naked, in pieces, in a trash dump somewhere. I'm not trying to be melodramatic — that's just the statistical average of victims in these kinds of circumstances. Anyway, there it is. What you decide is entirely your call."

"Later," Erika spoke up again. Chief Warner regained the podium.

"Next is Molly Rogers, the Building Supervisor, a high-priced name for your personal Keeper for the next few weeks while we're working on the case." Molly went to the podium and began her explanation.

"I'll show you the Visitor's Suite, as we call it, where you'll live for a while. We'll try to make you as comfortable as possible — television, radio, DVD player, meals of your choice, nice bedrooms, good view of the city, nice furniture, a kind of high priced hotel suite. There's only one catch. Your door will always be locked with a digital keypad, and you can never leave except for extraordinary reasons.

There are two couriers at your beckon. They get your meals, go to the store for you, and look in on you four times a day. The couriers are changed once a week. They all carry picture badges and guns. You can call for them using a special device I'll give you later. You are not to have any conversation with them. Whatever you want will have to be written down on a piece of paper and passed through a special locked opening in the door to your room. There's still more, but I'll explain at a later time.

This has been a long meeting, so let's break off. Miss Stevens, I have a badge you'll need to wear at all times. Everyone knows who you are so if they catch you wandering the halls you'll right away be wearing handcuffs. Sorry, but we just can't afford to be too careful."

Erika sighed and stood up. "Guess I've really put my foot in it this time," she complained, then turning toward Marc, she said, "Will I ever see you again, Marc? I was just beginning to rely on you."

Marc laughed quietly. "I'm going to stick to you like glue, honey. Whatever we have going between us is pretty nice, and I want to get to know you much better. We've confiscated your cell phone – you'll have to use the room phone, but you still have my number. No, I'll just be a breath away. Maybe tonight I'll come and tuck you into bed. Would you like that?" Without commenting, she looked at him with a slight smile as they all left the room.

Sitting at Chief Warner's private conference table, Erika and Marc were surrounded by FBI and other law enforcement agents including Molly Rogers. Chief Warner opened the discussion.

"I've had several discussions by telephone with Ian Brooks, Chief Inspector of Scotland Yard in London. He, in turn, has been discussing our situation with Britain's MI6 group, Interpol and our American FBI. All of us have arrived at a very simplified but very important solution to Miss Stevens' problems, and we would like to go over the solution with both of you. Here's what we propose.

Marc has had several months' training at Britain's MI6 special training school in the north of England. The Brits know Marc and have been very impressed with the level of his skills. Scotland Yard's Ian Brooks would like to bring Marc to London to help with their investigation of what is now recognized as an international group of criminals. Are you all with me so far? There's more." Chief Warner looked around the room and noted that everyone was in agreement.

"Good, now let's get to the nuts and bolts of all this," he said. "With assistance from the American government, Marc's salary will be raised slightly, and will be matched with funds from the British government. Since Miss Stevens can never go back to her old job, and since she was/is the initial witness to what has transpired so far in this country, we suggest that she accompany Marc.

Her salary will be set by the British government and matched by the American government. This plan will give the Brits an additional expert investigator as well as the added benefit of Miss Stevens' experience. And. . .we'll get Miss Stevens out of the country and off to England where Europeans don't know her. How does all this sit with each of you?"

Marc and Erika both accepted the new assignments. Marc looked at her with a twinkle in his eye; Erika looked over at him with a slight smile as she realized both of them would be working closely together. They left the meeting to make their plans for the future.

In the middle of the week, Marc's phone jangled early on a Wednesday morning. Chief Warner immediately spoke in a flurry of words. "Marc, get over here to my office fast, something suspicious is going on and I'm concerned about Erika's safety. Make it quick."

Once inside, Marc didn't bother to sit down. "You sound like you're in a panic," he queried the Chief, "What's going on?"

"Look outside the window. See that telephone lineman? What's he doing up there?" Warner asked.

"He's just fixing the telephone lines," Marc coughed, "Chief, I think you're getting paranoid – you see a street punk behind every lamp post."

"I've been watching him," the Chief continued, "he's not fixing anything, he's disconnecting some of the phone lines. Get out there and get him down, Marc, before he gets away."

In the street below, Marc called up to the lineman. "Come on down here a minute, fella, I wanna talk to you, and I wanna see your identification."

On the ground, the lineman seemed impatient. "Jeez, you cops are always nervous about something. I was sent over here to clear up some static on the lines, what's wrong with that?"

"Telephone employees all carry badges, let me see your ID," Marc demanded again.

"Sure, buddy, let me get it out of my pocket." As the lineman's hand slid out of his overalls, Marc saw the unmistakable square outline of a pistol. Reaching for his own sidearm, Marc had just enough time to change position before the man got off one shot that missed Marc by only a few inches. Marc fired his own gun striking the lineman in the chest causing him to topple to the ground as two other officers came running out of the station.

"If this guy's a telephone lineman, I'm the Easter bunny," Marc snarled bending over the man. "Who are you and what are you doing here?" The man refused to talk. "You're dying, so whatever you have to say, you better say it quick. What are you doing here?" There was no answer, only the sound of the man's last breath.

Marc's radio crackled. "Marc, you better get up here quick, Erika's courier was just found dead at one of the back doors to the station, which means that lineman cut her phone wire and someone's on the way to the visitor suite. They're going after her again and we better get there first. I've sent two officers up to the suite."

Marc didn't bother to answer as he broke into a dead run for the elevator. *Desperate again*, he thought, *they must really want to get her.* As the elevator doors opened, he heard shots being fired. Rounding a corner, he found a woman lying on the floor beside one wounded officer and another officer leaning against the wall. The smell of gunpowder was everywhere and he could hear Erika shouting and pounding on the wall inside the suite. Sizing up the scene, he unlocked the door to find Erika sobbing. They embraced, trying to comfort each other.

"Marc, why won't they stop, they keep trying to kill me? How did this happen?"

"We'll keep you safe, don't worry," Marc told her.

"That's what all of you said before, but it isn't working. The police got here just in time, maybe they won't get here fast enough next time. I have to get out of here, Marc, there's no place to hide. Where can we go?"

Chief Warner reached the room momentarily. "I'm so sorry, Miss Stevens," he apologized, "evidently they're bent on getting to you, but I think I have a way out of this. Sit down for a few minutes and let's talk. I didn't quite realize how intent they are, and their attempts are becoming more complex. First, we'll post two guards up here, one at the elevator and the other outside your door. The Brits are calling a conference for the end of the week, including Scotland Yard, MI6, Interpol and the French. They want Marc to be there along with you.

Here's how this ought to play out, Erika. We'll put you in a disguise and send you along with Marc. You're the only witness in this scenario. One of the girls downstairs will help change your appearance - hair color and style, different clothing, and so forth. We'll get you to London and let the Brits put you to work. This gang has a very far-reaching influence, and it's extremely well organized. But we're missing something here in this country. Maybe the Europeans will come up with something new. We also need a tight tie-in with Interpol.

The gang is running weapons, drugs, works of art such as paintings and jewelry, and probably other things we can only guess at. Their operation is enormous, reaching America, Europe and South America. If we all of us pool our resources, we're bound to find a weakness in their operation. We'll set up a command post with lines of communication that we all feed into, that way we'll cover most of the globe. The Europeans agree that this is our best chance. In the meantime, we'll get Miss Stevens out of the country and over to Europe where she'll be safe and can make a contribution."

4

Off Trafalgar Square at London's Scotland Yard, Chief Inspector Ian Brooks leaned back in his desk chair and stared into space. Glancing back once more at the paper in his hand, he began thinking far ahead. Then he reached for the telephone and buzzed his secretary. "Miss Worthington, ask Inspector Childers to step into my office, please. Tell him it's serious business, we need to make some immediate decisions. Also tell him I'm sorry to break up his day, but we have a priority issue brewing."

Derek Childers sat uncomfortably in his chair and looked over at Inspector Brooks expectantly. "What's in the wind, Ian, your secretary sounded serious."

"It is at that, Derek," Ian furrowed his brow, "the Americans are on alert and I'm calling a full Director's conference for this one. I'm off the phone with the American FBI about this cable that just came in. I think there's a break in a case we first had wind of a year ago, in St. Louis, in the States.

The FBI has the point in America; they've named it *Operation Lady Luck* and have already assigned some codes to certain aspects. I'm also calling the French in on this conference, as well as our MI6 group and Interpol. The French have assigned several agencies – first is the DGSE, the *direction generale de la securite exterieure*, the DGSI *direction generale de la securite interieure*, and the DCPJ *direction centrale de la police judiciaire*. These three agencies will be monitoring Interpol, Scotland Yard, and the American FBI. Don't let the French language put you off, just be aware that the French consider this gang of criminals to be an internal and external threat. The French always do a very competent job in matters like this one and you can have full confidence in them.

This is going to be a good sized international investigation and we need to get prepared as quickly as possible. If the original gang of druggies and gunrunners is involved, and I think it is, the case could break wide open all across the continent at any moment."

"Well, I think you might be right," Derek assured, "what did you learn from the FBI?"

Chief Inspector Brooks went over his entire conversation with Special Agent Dobson in Washington, including photographs faxed to London, emphasizing how well it all seemed organized.

"The Americans are stuck on the *'Mr. Lambert'* thing just like we are. It's obviously a code word of some sort, but no one knows anything about it. I'll leave the gathering of eagles to you, Derek, say about nine thirty the day after tomorrow morning? In the meantime, I'll contact the French and the MI6 group, you call in Interpol.

Better tell everyone lunch is on us tomorrow," Brooks continued, "the conference no doubt will take the whole day, maybe more. No media on this one, total media blackout, we don't want to tip off our hand. I'm also asking the Americans to send over Lieutenant Marcus Edwards from the Manchester PD – this case is going to need his special talents. Marc has an unusual set of talents and now he has a good grip on the background that occurred in St. Louis. He has much to contribute."

At the London conference, Marc and Erika were seated at a huge table with some 20 representatives from at least as many law enforcement agencies. FBI Special Agent John Dobson turned over the point to Ian Brooks of Scotland Yard who issued a position paper about lines of communication and procedure, and the conference got underway. After breaking for lunch later, they reconvened for four afternoon hours of discussion. It was working; the group was now prepared to make a reasonable amount of progress.

Sherlock Holmes Restaurant and Museum, London

"The Sherlock Holmes Restaurant is only a couple of blocks down the street," Marc suggested, looking at Erika, "we can get an excellent dinner and talk about the day's events. How does that sound? It's very appropriate for the work we're doing, a quaint old place, even has a Sherlock museum upstairs. I think you'll like it."

"Oh, that sounds really interesting," Erika became excited. "I liked reading Sherlock Holmes, even watched a lot of movies about his exploits, especially the 'Hound of the Baskervilles' which was how I first became interested in Sherlock Holmes."

Over dinner, they discussed the conference and the tourist sites about London. "I'd like to see a few of the more common places," Erika offered. "I've never been to London and I don't want to go home saying all I saw was a conference room and the inside of a hotel."

"You've already seen two of the most important tourist sites," Marc said. "When we arrived, we passed through the Victoria Bus Station of the Sherlock Holmes stories. It's known all over the world. Anyway, we can manage some sightseeing, I think," Marc said, looking over at her.

"History is about to come alive for you-all those places you read about in your history classes. They were just pictures in a book, but now they'll suddenly become real. I envy you, there's nothing quite as exciting as a new discovery."

"I'm beginning to realize that," Erika agreed, but with a meaning different from the one Marc referred to. For Erika, her greatest discovery was meeting Marc; the second greatest discovery for her was actually falling in love with him.

Victoria Bus Station/Train Station

"You could spend a month in London and not see the same thing twice," Marc went on. He reached over and put his hand on hers. It wasn't just a reassuring touch. Erika sensed it had a deeper feeling to it. Their eyes met momentarily and for both of them, there was a feeling of bonding that went beyond simply getting to know each other. They were working together at last, which made getting to know each other better that much more enjoyable.

"I'm very proud of you, Erika. You've stood up to all this like a champion in spite of the shocks and hazards. You're quite a girl – I'm starting to have some very real feelings about you that I don't quite know what to do with. Since I've been reassigned to work with Scotland Yard, we'll be here for quite some time, and I've worked out an agreement for us with Ian Brooks.

She purposely switched the conversation when he said *worked out an agreement*. She immediately wondered what an agreement meant. Surely he wouldn't get her involved in something without checking with her first. "Do you like my new hair-do? Do I look alright as a dark-haired girl?" she asked.

Marc chuckled. "I'd like you if your hair was green," he said.

Their eyes met again. Erika became aware of her own feelings that went beyond the need for protection from a man who warmed her heart. A dozen times a day she surveyed her changing, and growing, attitude toward him. Now she saw him as a warm and capable partner who shared something more than the earlier need only for survival.

He was a man of strong character, she decided - educated, curious, watchful in ways that seemed to show he truly might care for her as she cared for him. Yes, there was an excitement about new discoveries. Aside, she hoped these new feelings were real for both of them. Then her thoughts were interrupted by Marc's radio.

"Marc, this is Derek from Scotland Yard, something has happened. Can you and Erika get over to the office here? Things are starting to heat up."

"We'll be right there, we're just down the street a ways."

"Good, we're waiting for you. Out"

Marc reached for the dinner bill. "Here we go. Didn't take very long, did it?"

"A break in the case?" she assumed.

"I suppose," he replied, "we'll know when we get there."

"Two paintings were stolen from the St. Louis Art Museum and one of the guards was killed - a Monet Impressionist and a Wyeth winter scene – worth a fortune," Chief Inspector Brooks started off.

"I think this international gang just made a big blunder," Brooks added. "The public isn't aware that the Monet has a homing chip hidden in the frame. Right now, Chief Warner and the FBI know exactly where the paintings are, we can follow their course geographically. Let's hope we'll get some sleep tonight."

Houses of Parliament, London

"Not much sleep," Brooks ventured, "there are a lot of questions we don't have answers for. For example, why St. Louis, why choose this laid-back mid-western town? And why are these ruffians so intent on getting Miss Stevens out of the way? Explain those questions for a start. What possible kind of threat could she be now?"

Brooks' overseas telephone began to jangle. "Scotland Yard," he answered. There was a long pause until the Chief Inspector began to speak.

"Can you get a detective there right away?" he said quickly. Another long pause. Brooks again: "I need as much detail as possible to decide how they're operating. Take plenty of pictures, but don't touch anything, I'll call you back." With a frown, Brooks looked up at the two of them.

"They've also struck at your home guard, your National Guard unit I think you call it, in Kansas City – made off with thirty AK47s and a large amount of ammunition and hand guns. Luckily no one was injured, and this is curious, they used chloroform on the only man that was on guard. They broke in by cutting all the wires going into the building. The guard had no notice they were on the premises until he woke up this morning, and by the way, the FBI is already on the scene." Brooks put the phone back on its cradle.

"Sounds like the hit was very carefully staged," Marc suggested. Erika joined in at that point. "Why Kansas City?" she wondered out loud, "There really isn't much there for them."

Marc raised up straight in his chair. "That's the point," he said, smacking his hands together, "it's a really easy hit with no witnesses. They just pulled their trucks to the door and loaded up. I bet they were gone in less than fifteen minutes. It was a commando raid."

Brooks rubbed his chin. "That's a departure from all the other robberies," he frowned, "because it was so easy. For an international gang, no muss no fuss as you Americans say. How convenient!"

Erika sank back into her chair studying the tips of her shoes. Considering the simplicity of the theft, she wondered why the thieves bothered at all. Surely guns, drugs, unique artifacts would bring more money into the gang's bank account. "Is this the start of something?" she wondered out loud, "it's pretty weak, don't you think?"

"That's it, by Jove, old girl, I think you've hit on something," Brooks stammered, jumping to his feet. "It's not the main event – it's a diversion to lead us away from what's really about to happen. We need to get Derek and his team in on this."

Saying that, Brooks reached for the phone, waking Derek out of a sound sleep.

"Let's go, old boy, get your team moving, the roof just caved in on us. Call in your whole team and get them on the telephones phoning the French, the Dutch, the Germans, Interpol, MI6, everyone. Something's about to break loose. Alert the British

Museum and the National Gallery here in London and the Louvre in Paris." Marc noticed his watch showed 11:20pm. "There goes tonight's sleep," he made a sour face.

"Erika, you don't have to stay here," Marc suggested, "why don't you go back to the hotel and get some rest? I'll wake you in the morning."

She refused his offer with a slight snicker. "I'm not going anywhere without you," she countered, "they're liable to go after me right here in London. I don't trust anybody but you, dear."

Marc smiled. "There's a day-bed in the next room, why don't you stretch out, I'll let you know when the fur starts to fly."

"Nothing doing," she answered again, "if you can stand it, so can I."

"Marc, you take MI6, Erika you call Interpol - Administrator Pierre Champole," Brooks directed, "get 'em going out on the streets. Tell 'em to check in with me when they're on station. We want to cover every possibility. Use the phone on that desk over there," he motioned. "Hopefully, we'll catch someone. Now comes the tough part – waiting for something to break loose. They know we're on to them, so it's too late for that."

Within an hour, all stations had checked in with Brooks and the net was ready to spring. The minutes passed slowly. By one o'clock, the action phones were still silent. More minutes slowly slipped by. At 1:30, the first call came in.

"We killed two and captured two, with about half a million Euros in diamonds, in downtown Amsterdam," the voice said. "We're processing all this as we speak. I'll call you back when I have something we can work on." In a few moments, another call came in.

The Rosetta Stone, British Museum, London

"Nick Federer at Interpol at the Isle de la Citie de Paris," the voice announced. "We caught some fools trying to steal objects from the Notre Dame cathedral, about seven priceless goblets, a painting, and some rare manuscripts. I'll call back when we have a substantial report for you."

Two phones rang at once, one from the Dutch Rijksmuseum in Amsterdam and the other from the British Black Watch Guard in Edinburgh, Scotland. The Rijksmuseum Director was in a rage.

"How dare they steal from us," he shouted in the phone at Marc, "and to go off in the middle of the night with one of the world's premier art works! The ignorant bastards, do they think they can steal from us like street ruffians?"

Marc tried to assuage his anger but without success. "What did they take from you, Director?"

"The Night Watch, The Night Watch," he stammered over and over again.

Marc lowered his voice. "How did they accomplish that?" he asked, almost on the verge of laughing out loud.

"Through the front door, they broke it down, right off the wall," the Director shouted, "killed one of my guards and used a twelfth century living room couch, too. Your Interpol man has all the details. I want that painting back now! Go after those common gutter bugs, get my painting back, put them in jail for the rest of their lives!"

"You keep saying 'they', Director," Marc followed up. "How do you know it was more than one person?"

"The note, the note, they left it on the floor below where the painting was hanging, too big for only one person – must have been three or four. The painting's huge, twelve feet by fourteen feet."

"And what did the note say?" Marc continued.

"Here, here, I read it to you. It says 'The Night Watch doesn't watch very well.'"

Marc almost burst into laughter. "Seems like they have a sense of humor, Director."

"Naw, naw, is not funny, not crude joke," the Director concluded, "get my painting back!"

"We're doing everything we can, Director, I'll keep you informed." Marc hung up the phone and leaned back in his chair, smiling. If it wasn't so tragic, it could almost be a hilarious joke.

"Well, that's one for the record books, the thieves left a note," Marc called over to Erika who already was on the phone with another break-in.

The Night Watch, Rembrandt, Rijksmuseum, Amsterdam

Brooks hung up his phone and simply sat in his chair staring out the window. The many colored lights of downtown London seemed especially to twinkle at him, as if to join in the joke. "What's wrong, Ian?" Marc looked over, wiping his eyes from the sting of lack of sleep.

"I'm not sure," Brooks lamented, "but this is all too perfect, too coordinated, too everything. It's the greatest robbery in history. That was the Bishop of the Cologne Cathedral in Germany. They tied him up but he managed to get loose. The buggers looted the church — altarpieces, paintings, collection boxes, and they even pried loose the ornate metal artwork on the front door. It took 'em three hours to gut the cathedral. What are they going to do with all that stuff?"

Marc leaned back in his chair, calculating. "Let's see now, half a million euros in diamonds and one of the world's most celebrated paintings, the Night Watch, which measures about 12 X 14 feet, all in Amsterdam. Next, they looted the altar at Notre Dame Cathedral in Paris. Then there's the National Guard unit in Kansas City, AK47s, handguns and ammunition, and some priceless paintings from the St. Louis Art Museum. What comes next?"

Chief Inspector Brook's phone rang again and he reached for it with a dreaded premonition.

"Yes, this is Chief Inspector Ian Brooks of Scotland Yard, who am I speaking to?" he asked. After a short silence, he acknowledged the caller. "Yes, yes, I see, talk slower, please, you're going too fast." A longer silence this time as Brooks slapped his knee.

"This is the Vice President of the National Gallery of Art," the voice continued, "we've been robbed of twelve priceless manuscripts plus three paintings that are national treasures. They simply smashed the glass cases and lifted the manuscripts out. The paintings were carried out the front door while men with machine guns held the guards at bay. They all wore white masks and dark running clothes. Luckily no one was injured. They also cut all the electric and telephone wires. What do you make of this, Chief Inspector?"

Restored Medieval Town of Rothenburg, Germany

"It's quite a mystery," Brooks confessed, "but it's been happening all over Europe, and all at the same time. We'll know more by end of day tomorrow, but right now we're making determinations about coordination, choices of stolen objects, and so forth, looking for patterns of activity. We'll let you know when we have something substantial."

Erika looked at her watch and saw that it read 3:15 in the morning. She yawned and tried to register a weak smile at Marc. "I'm going to collapse if this continues much longer," she said with a shiver. "I think I'll take you up on that day-bed in the next room."

She slowly lifted herself out of her chair and headed for the door, Marc following behind her into the makeshift sleeping room.

"I'll look in on you once in a while, hon." They stood studying each other for a few moments. Deciding to be bold, Erika spoke up first.

"I know what you're thinking – you'd like to be in that bed with me, wouldn't you?"

"Honey, I. . ." Stepping closer to him, she stopped him in mid-sentence.

"I can't believe this, Marc, but I feel like I'm falling in love with you. I've watched you closely, how you work, how you think, how considerate you are toward me, and it's admirable. I've had lots of dates, but that's all they were, just dates with men who either wanted to get me in bed or men who were just taking a break from life, just tolerating me. I've never met a man I felt I'd like to be close to, with his arms around me. In fact, I've never been in love before; it's a brand new experience for me, kind of unsettling."

Marc stood glued to the floor. "I feel the same way, Erika, like you're the woman I've been waiting for my whole life."

He moved over in front of her putting his arms around her waist. She felt warm and soft, and suddenly he was kissing her and pulling her tighter against him. She moved backward slightly and stood staring.

"I can hardly breathe, and I want to kiss you again. Oh. . .why does it have to be three o'clock in the morning, and in this place? Kiss me again, Marc, and then leave before I get all worked up. And please stay close to me."

They encircled each other for several more minutes. He put his hand on the side of her face and caressed her hair.

"I'd better go, I'm getting upset, too," Marc said. "I'll check on you at intervals." Heading for the door, he turned for one last look at her, then left the room. What a weird time to fall in love, he thought.

Front Door Metal Artwork, Cologne Cathedral, Germany

The mega-thefts continued to build. From Edinburgh came reports of a theft at the armory of the Black Watch military unit. Missing things much like the theft at Kansas City's National Guard armory were thirty AK47 repeating rifles and ammunition, not a large heist but significant. The thieves even made off with the cannon at Edinburgh Castle used to announce the noon hour. Following were more thefts at intervals during the night until the total haul amounted to many millions of dollars and euros.

At 4:45am, Marc, Ian and Derek were nearing the end of the closely timed theft operations. They drafted a lengthy report and sent it to each of the international law enforcement agencies. Marc went into the makeshift sleeping room where he tumbled into bed beside Erika, totally exhausted. He had to push Erika aside to lie down. Kissing her softly, he knew the next day would be just as exhausting when they sifted through all the reports looking for patterns and pieces of stray information.

In the morning, however, Ian called another grand conference of law enforcement at Scotland Yard headquarters, which found him once more standing at the podium ready to close the conference at noon. Erika raised her hand and looked up at Ian.

"Besides an opportunity for bragging," she reminded the assemblage, "I think you might question another summary of all the thefts. I think the thieves are making a statement of some kind."

Ian's head jerked up and he squinted at her briefly. "I say, good show, Miss Stevens, a very good point. What makes you think so?"

"All the gang's activities in the States," she said, "seem to emphasize the same thought over and over again. Isn't the gang saying, *look what we can do and you can't catch us*? Altogether several gang members were killed, but only one person was captured and he isn't talking. Don't you think all that's unusual?"

"Could you stay after the meeting for a moment, Miss Stevens?"

Ian sauntered over to her. "Let's go back to that day when you discovered your friend had been murdered. You saw two men coming in the door behind you. Did you see anyone else that day?"

Erika thought for a few seconds. "Out of the corner of my eye I thought I saw a man across the street get out of his car," Erika said. "It was very fuzzy and I was in shock so I can't be absolutely certain. It was just a second of a glimpse, but yes, I think I saw a third man."

"Would you recognize that man if you saw him again?" Ian pressed onward.

"I doubt it, because I didn't feel threatened by him, so I dismissed it," Erika mused.

Ian studied her for several seconds. "Have you ever been hypnotized, Miss Stevens?" She shook her head. "No, do you think that would help me recognize him?"

I think it's worth a try," Ian nodded. "Sit down a minute, I'll get Doctor Wentworth."

Marc came into the room yawning and scratching his head. "What's this about hypnotized? And where's the coffee pot?"

The doctor arrived and prepared Erika for hypnosis, sitting across from her at a small table, then he went to work using his watch as a pendulum. "Close your eyes and listen to the sound of my voice; you'll start feeling sleepy. Keep your mind on my voice and relax," the doctor went on. "Let your mind go back in time to the day you discovered Susan's Art Shop ransacked. Can you see yourself entering the door? Two men with guns are close behind you. You glance at the front of the store – what else do you see – right now – now, at this moment?" Erika squirmed for a second.

"Do you see him – the third man?" the doctor kept up the pace, "what kind of clothing is he wearing, what color, what does he look like?"

"Brown jacket – bald head – moustache – blue pants – shielding his eyes from the sun – looking in through the window." Erika stopped, then began to squirm in her chair becoming more and more agitated. "It's wrong, the room is wrong, messy, and. . ." suddenly she cried out. "Oh no, Susan. . ." she whimpered wringing her hands, "what did you do?"

Immediately the doctor explained to those in the room that he didn't want to take her through the discovery scene once more because it brought back memories of Susan lying dead on the floor.

"Erika, do you hear my voice now; this is Doctor Wentworth?" he asked. "Yes," she replied.

"I'm going to count backward from five and you will wake up. "Five- four – three – two – one – you're waking up now."

Erika swayed back and forth in the chair, then opened her eyes. She had been starting to cry but now she was awake looking at the doctor. "Was it a dream?" she asked, still wringing her hands.

"Good girl, Erika," Marc touched her shoulder. "What a break in the case this is. Honey, you did great, you won't believe what you just discovered."

"Is your memory better now?" the doctor probed. "Do you think you could describe the man you saw? We'll get a sketch artist up here and you can talk to her."

After an hour or so, the artist showed Marc and Ian what she had drawn. "It's not picture perfect, but it's close," the artist praised Erika. "I don't think she can do any better."

Marc suddenly closed his eyes and clenched his fists. "That's it, that's why they've been after her," he said excitedly, "because they think she can identify the third man. If it's true, they won't stop 'til they get to her − because he's probably the brain behind the whole operation. But what was he doing in St. Louis when the gang is more European?"

Rhine River Watch Tower and Lighthouse, Germany

Go back to your hotel," Ian smiled briefly, "you're both exhausted, especially Erika. Take a few days off, you've earned it, leave this mess to Scotland Yard for awhile. I'll call you on Tuesday so you can have several days to yourselves."

"Great idea," Marc agreed. "We both need some rest. Come on, honey, let's go."

With that, they gathered their belongings and left. At the hotel, they stumbled into Marc's room. After a moment or two, they rushed into each other's arms and shared hungry kisses.

"Marc, do you realize we haven't had a minute to ourselves? I don't even know if you already have a girlfriend," she commented breathlessly. Then she announced in complete surprise, "I'll race you getting undressed," she laughed as she unbuttoned her blouse and slipped out of it along with her bra.

"No, I don't have a girlfriend," he volunteered. "What about you, do you have a partner?"

"No, no boyfriend," she said. "Just never met the right guy until you came along." Her voice became soft and velvety as she faced him across the room

"I'm not very experienced, you'll have to show me how all this is done." There was a moment of silence. "You'll be kind to me, Marc, won't you? It's been such a long time since I've been with a man, and even then it wasn't a very good experience."

"Well of course I'll be kind," Marc said calmly, "I've always been kind to you, because I love you." Suddenly Marc stood open-mouthed. He realized he said it out loud for the whole world to hear, a wonderful confession he hadn't even allowed him to say to himself.

"I know you do," she mumbled, "I'm so happy to hear you say it. I guess I'm just nervous. It's our first time."

Her clothes were off now and she turned full forward toward him. Marc looked over at her, involuntarily catching his breath.

"You're so beautiful, Erika, so absolutely beautiful."

"Are my breasts too small for you, honey? I haven't been naked in front of a man for a very long time. I don't want to disappoint you, but it's been a long time since I did this."

"They're perfect, just like the rest of you," he said softly. "We won't disappoint each other, don't worry about that. Once you learn you never forget," Marc reminded her. "Besides, it all comes naturally."

Marc caressed her body and took in the whole of her as he wrapped his arms about her.

"I'm so proud of you, Erika," he murmured, "and the way you took the lead at the conference this morning. I love you with all my heart, and I always will."

They came together, locked in an embrace and exploring each other's body, shutting off the world around them as they gave in to their love making, surrendering to the feelings for each other that had been building steadily for several months. The afternoon slowly became fuzzy and drifted away as they both became one and swam in the togetherness that only comes with the joy of first love. Her breath was warm against his shoulder as she snuggled up to him. They began to stir after an hour or so.

"Let's get dressed, I know a place where no one will know who we are," Marc began. "We can be there in time for supper, then we'll have a few days to just unwind. You're going to love it there, just the two of us in this perfect little village in Wales called Tenby. We'll take the British fast train most of the way and get there in a couple of hours in time to watch the brilliant sunset."

By suppertime, they were having their meal by candlelight in a quaint restaurant by the open sea. "What do you think of this little town?" Marc asked.

"It's gorgeous, and I'll never forget today for the rest of my life," she cooed. "Let's call this our own private hideaway."

"We'll just have time to get over to the harbor before the sun goes down and the tide comes in. You're right, this is idyllic, almost a dream," Marc agreed. "Tenby is going to be our secret getaway forever."

For several days of freedom, they explored the village and each other, getting to know each other better and better, closely sharing their newly found discoveries. Strolls on the beach, finding little souvenirs in the marketplace, holding hands as they strolled along the cliffs, it all became a journey through the beginning of a new life. At Tuesday noon, Marc's phone rang. Reluctantly, he answered to hear Ian's familiar voice.

"Marc, I really dislike having to bring you and Erika back to all this, but we've made a great deal of progress. You're going to be amazed, and the international law enforcement agencies are working nicely together. Be in my office first thing tomorrow morning – and don't forget to bring your genius along. We're going to need her expert help, she has an unusual perspective on all this."

"We'll be there, put the coffee pot on. See you then."

"I say, old boy, what do you have against good British tea?"

"I don't know, guess we dumped it all in Boston Harbor, but that's another story for another day. Cheerio."

★ ★ ★

"We managed to capture one of the hoodlums; rather, Interpol did, but he's still not talking," Ian pointed out. "Somehow we have to get him to open up. Kinda surly, actually, I thought you might be able to get him started. Interrogation is one of your specialties."

"Do you have a name for him?" Marc inquired. "We need to start with that so we can get personal with him quicker."

Ian scratched his head. "We think his name is Marcel, a Frenchman, but we're not absolutely certain. Have a go at him, Marc - Erika and I'll stay behind the mirror."

"Did you empty his pockets, are there any clues there?"

Ian breathed a sigh of frustration. "All he had on him was a driver license, in French and in German both, but they could be forged. He had a pack of cigarettes, several sticks of gum, a pocket knife and a pocket comb, but not even a wallet."

Boat Harbor, Tenby, Wales

Marc casually walked into the interrogation room and sat down across from the man. *"M'apelle est monsieur Marc Edwards. Quel est votre nom? Quell age avez vous?"*

The man simply stared at Marc without a word. *"Parlez vous Anglais, monsieur?"* Marc asked, pulling his chair closer to the table between them. Still no response. Marc laid the man's driver licenses on the table.

"We have several charges against you," Marc began to bear down a little harder. "International theft, murder, conspiracy to commit murder, accessory to murder, evading arrest, refusal to cooperate with law enforcement, and a few more lesser charges, take your pick. That's enough right there to put you in jail for a number of years, especially the charge of premeditated murder.

You'd better come clean if you don't want to spend the next twenty-five years in jail. Do you understand what I'm saying?"

"I didn't kill anybody," Marcel spat out the words. Marc detected just a hint of a British accent. So under duress, Marcel was British, not French, and his English was almost perfect.

"Maybe, maybe not, but you were there when he was killed," Marc pressed on. "You were a party to it, weren't you, that makes you an accessory to murder and part of the conspiracy to theft. You'd better tell us what you know, Marcel, if that's really your name. In any event, your life is over, you'll never see the streets again. In fact, you'll never feel the sun on your face again, or watch the moon rise in the early evening."

"They'll kill me," Marcel responded. "No matter what I do or where I go, they'll get me, monsieur." Marc was pleased with his interrogation. Now it was time to spring the trap.

Tenby street scene, Wales

"You know, we could reduce your sentence somewhat if you cooperate with us. Who's Mr. Lambert?"

The man suddenly went white faced and he began to squirm in his chair. Behind the mirror, Erika murmured quietly, "Marc's got him now. He's going to sing for us, isn't he?"

Ian and Derek both smiled. "Marc's good, we picked the right man to interrogate," Derek affirmed. "This hooligan's scared to death now."

"The reduced sentence is on the table and the clock is ticking, Marcel. What's it going to be, life in prison or maybe only a few years? It's a one-time offer, take it or leave it."

"I. . .I can't," Marcel whined, "I'm telling you they'll kill me. They'll even get to me in prison if I tell you."

Marc took out the artist's sketch of "Mr. Somebody" that Erika had helped create and slammed it down on the table in front of the man. "Who is this, Marcel? Is this Mr. Lambert? Is this who it is? What do you know about him? Time's slipping away."

"He's too powerful – he has people working for him all over Europe," Marcel said, and then became quiet once more.

"Is this a good likeness of Mr. Lambert?" Marc asked.

"Yes – but just a little thinner," Marcel answered quietly.

"Last chance, Marcel!" Marc spoke the words with authority, but the man refused to say anymore and the interrogation was over. Marc stood up, gathered his papers together, and walked to the door. Pausing a moment, he turned and looked at Marcel a last time. No, it was over and they had answers to a lot of questions.

"Good job, Marcus, I think we learned something," Derek prompted. "You fellows in the States have a different kind of interrogation technique than we do here, a little rougher than us."

"We need to get to the truth faster, maybe," Marc replied. "Okay, we have some work to do. Call the artist back and have her make whatever changes are necessary so that he looks a little thinner and fill in so he looks more three dimensional," Marc requested. "In the meantime, it's possible Lambert is British. Let's run his revised sketch through a subject identification screening, ask Interpol and MI6 to do the same. What else did we learn?"

Swiss Alps (Mosses Pass) near Interlaken

Ian thought a moment, then added, "We're on the right track thinking the gang is truly global, and that Lambert can be brutal if he can get to anyone anywhere. He must have connections all over the world. His organizational skills are impeccable and he definitely is feared all over the world."

Within an hour of circulating the revised sketch of Mr. Lambert, Interpol called Ian with a positive ID on the sketch that also was confirmed by America's Central Intelligence Agency.

"His full name is Phillip George Lambert," the Interpol intelligence group confirmed. "British passport but triple citizenships with France and Switzerland. Passport photos being faxed. Criminal records in France, Germany and Scotland for low level crimes, no record in the US, mostly lesser criminal activities of suspected robbery, suspected international drug and arms dealing, six months' jail time two years ago for attempted fraud. No convictions for felony crimes, though."

"I would have figured as much," Marc spoke up. "Marcel is an errand boy, certainly not at the top of the food chain, but Lambert IS at the top. In fact, he's probably the leader. Let's keep the press off this as much as possible, we don't want our catch murdered before we can get more information out of him. Your turn this time, Ian."

Suddenly bells went off all over the building. "That's an alarm in case something is wrong in the holding cells area," Ian shouted at Marc. "It usually means there's an attempted cell break. Stay here both of you, Marc, don't step out of this office."

Ian left the office at a dead run. Reaching the holding cells area, he found one of the prison guards on the floor in a pool of blood, yet all the cell doors were closed and locked. It was then he saw Marcel lying face up inside his cell with a knife protruding from his chest about where his heart is located. Rushing up to the scene, Derek stopped short when he realized what had happened. After a moment or two, Derek said out loud what everyone else was thinking.

"This is very serious, Ian, Marcel must have been killed by someone who had normal access to the holding area. You know what that means." Ian and Derek returned to Ian's office.

"Bad news, Marcus, you're not going to like this, but Marcel was just found murdered in his cell," Ian slammed a sheaf of papers down on his desk. "It was a knife job – no witnesses, no suspects, no one saw or heard anything. How the hell could this happen inside Scotland Yard?"

"You've got a mole inside your ranks," Mark suggested, "that's how Lambert continues his power choke, I'll bet."

"We got to Marcel quickly and dragged some information out of him in the nick of time," Derek said in a matter of fact way. "Yes – a mole, without a doubt."

Erika suddenly sat down hard. Her face looked like stone as she put her hand to her mouth. She looked over at Marc, staring intently at him. "If they got to him, they can get to me," she choked out the words. "Marc, what are we going to do? I don't stand a chance." She began to tremble.

Ian and Derek prepared her to leave the building by the side entrance, dressing her in a man's hat and trench coat because it was raining. "Sit up front with me," Ian said, "I'll drive with Derek and Marc in the back seat. I'm taking you to a safe house across town."

They all piled in the car and drove away quickly. After ten minutes, Ian warned everyone sternly, "We have company, definitely one car and maybe two. Everyone hold on tight." Ian sped up slightly, changing lanes frequently until he realized one of the chase cars was right behind them.

Without warning, a second car struck them full force right at the back doorway where Derek was sitting, sending pieces of glass throughout their car that now was in a wide spin. Almost simultaneously, the second chase car smashed full force into the front of their car from the same side. Ian fought the steering wheel although by now their car was entirely out of control sliding through an intersection. Marc heard police sirens arriving.

The assailants were pressing their advantage in a hail of bullets. Marc jumped out of the door on his side and, turning quickly, threw open Erika's door pulling her out and forcing her down onto the concrete. He was firing his gun at the assassins, pinning them down against their own cars. Ian also fired several volleys in the same direction.

The arriving police immediately engaged in a fierce firefight, driving the assailants away although by now two of their attackers lay dead and a third was badly wounded. Ian directed Erika and Marc into one of the police cars and they all sped off. Once more, Erika was nearly hysterical as Marc covered her with his own body. "Won't this ever stop?" Erika stuttered. "I thought it was going to be easier here in England, but it's no different than St. Louis."

"The closer we get to catching Lambert, the worse it will become," Marc reassured her, kissing her lightly. "This tells us that Lambert is in a panic now. He can't allow us to catch up to him."

"Derek's dead from the crash," Ian said, "he also was thrown out of the car, but I'll get us to the safe house without any trouble now. I need to get to a hospital, and Marc, you've been hit twice, I can see the blood all over your pants legs. Looks like Erika was the only one not injured."

"She'll be okay when she calms down," Marc confided, "and I'm truly sorry about Derek. I know how much you relied on him for a number of things. This kind of thing will stop only when we get Lambert, and I'm absolutely determined to get the bastard now. What about you, Ian, are you okay?"

"I'm fine, just hit in the lower arm, it's okay, I'm just shaken up a bit," Ian answered.

Marc held Erika tightly in his arms until she stopped shaking. "Don't worry, honey, we're going to take good care of you. This is a super secret safe house, reserved for people the British want to totally disappear. And there's a medical staff there to take care of these wounds."

"That's right," Ian chimed in, "it's never been breached — never even been suspected over the past ten years. Once we're in the garage, you'll be safe for as long as it takes. We've even hidden a few Prime Ministers here and a number of other government officials."

"I'm sorry I've become a burden, gentlemen, but those guys never stop," Erika moaned and snuggled still closer against Marc. "If it wasn't for you two, I'd be dead by now. I'm so sorry about Derek, he was a good man."

"It wasn't your fault, Erika," Ian reassured her, "and just remember, these hoodlums have turned this whole affair into an international threat. They're after entire governments. We need to get our hands around Mr. Lambert's total game plan and devise a way to shut him down."

"Once Erika is tucked away, we need to set up a game plan of our own, Ian," Marc contributed, "and I'm going after that arrogant son-of-a-bitch and put him away for good."

The police car finally turned into an unobtrusive, out of the way warehouse far removed from the Scotland Yard main headquarters. It was an ideal hiding place. After settling Erika into her new quarters, Ian and Marc were treated and bandaged and made ready to go back to work.

The building, hidden behind a façade of deteriorating look-alike buildings, was an ultra-modern compound. Windows were sealed and painted black. The first floor was a complete office structure set up to handle the everyday affairs of a business complex. Employees were bussed each day back and forth to take care of the day's police business.

The second floor was devoted to a modern hospital staff, living quarters for temporary housing of special visitors, and a cafeteria and recreation facilities. On the third floor were barracks for military personnel and storage areas for the entire complex including office supplies and high-grade military weapons.

"I have to leave you for a while, Erika," Marc said, "so we can devise a fool-proof plan of action. It's Scotland Yard's major priority now, even the military's main priority. This whole affair has got out of hand because we were taken by surprise, but not again."

Alone, the two of them kissed long kisses and hugged each other. "How will I know where you are, how will I know if you're alive or dead?" Erika grimaced. "I don't like this, darling. I'm going to spend every day worrying about you."

"Not to worry, love," Marc reassured her, "I'll be in contact with you almost every day. You have a secure telephone in your quarters here at the Yard Complex, and I'll do my best to talk to you each day. I'll be okay. Ian will assign code names for us all and we'll use them first before we can talk to each other. He's also going to put you to work as a computer guru to keep your mind off what is happening. Actually, it's time you start earning your salary."

Back at Scotland Yard headquarters once more, Marc stopped in at Ian's office. "I'm really sorry about Derek. I know you're going to miss him." Ian studied Marc for a moment.

"Sit down, Marc, let's chat a few minutes." After they were settled, Ian started the discussion.

"Let's talk about this attack, I think there's more than one motive to it. Let's call them motive one, motive two, and so forth. I think motive one was to kill Derek, motive two was to kill Erika, and motive three was to totally destroy the car and everyone in it. What do you think, Marc?"

Downtown Lucerne early morning

"Why would killing Derek be the primary motive?" Marc questioned. "Everyone in the car provided a motive, why do you think Derek was part of the *primary* motive?"

"There's someone I'd like you to meet," Ian said. "He's standing out in the hall, let me wave him in. I think you'll find him a very interesting chap, I've known him for a number of years. His name is Charles Foxx. Don't let his appearance put you off."

Foxx came in and stood next to Marc a moment. Marc cleared his nose a few times and put out his hand. "Glad to meet you, Marc," Foxx thrust out his hand and Marc shook it lightly. At first glance, Marc was genuinely taken back by the man's unkempt appearance. He obviously had not shaved for several days and displayed a crusty beard along with every indication he hadn't bathed for at least a week. His stringy hair was down almost to his shoulders and hadn't been cut for months. His dirty fingernails hadn't been trimmed, either.

"This miserable misfit is an agent of our MI6 intelligence group, that's why he looks like a street knocker. Don't let his appearance fool you, Marc, he's one of MI6's best agents. He'd like to tell you a story."

"Yes, indeed," Foxx pulled his chair closer to the desk, "but don't be too surprised at what I'm going to say. Derek Childers was NOT the unfortunate victim of a traffic accident. He was carefully murdered right in front of you. You see, actually he was a mole, planted in Scotland Yard by Mr. Lambert a long time ago. What seemed to be an attack on Miss Stevens was Lambert's method of getting rid of Derek before he could be exposed for the idiot he was. We've been on to him for almost a year, but he knew a great deal about Lambert's organization, and Lambert was afraid he'd give up the organization's secrets under interrogation.

"I'm stunned down to my shoelaces," Marc confessed. "This is quite an evening, believe me, but couldn't Lambert kill him off in a different way? I mean, a car crash is a pretty spectacular weapon."

"Not at all, Marc," Ian put in. "You see, Lambert figured he could get rid of Derek and Miss Stevens both at once – two birds with one stone as you Americans say, and maybe even you and I to boot. We recognized the stunt immediately and had to get Miss Stevens away as fast as we could. Derek was very intelligent and we decided we couldn't tell you about him for fear your involuntary actions might make him suspicious we were on to him."

"Well, now I've heard it all," Marc said smiling.

"I'm afraid you haven't," Foxx began again. "Those two henchmen of Lambert's in the lockup were killed by Derek's hand. Lambert was afraid they'd talk under pressure from Scotland Yard. I thought they would, too. It's a shame Derek got to them before we could pull some good information out of them."

Foxx stood up at that point and indicated he had to get back on the street before he needed to explain why he was dragged into Scotland Yard for so long a time.

"Maybe sometime we'll meet when I don't look so bedraggled." Turning toward Ian, Foxx resumed his disguise. "Can you get a uniformed officer to push me out the front door? Have to keep up appearances, you know."

When Foxx was gone, Ian apologized for not telling Marc sooner about Derek. "Derek was getting careless, most of his work was getting shoddy and it was only a matter of time before we gave him the sac."

Marc went to work on his part of the response plan. Halfway in the midst of his studies, Ian burst into his office, stood with his hands on his hips and growled at Marc.

"They just struck at the armory in the Netherlands, in Amsterdam," Ian snarled. "It was a lightning quick raid, but they got away with fifteen shoulder firing missile weapons. That's the first we've heard of this kind of weapon. What do you think of that?"

"How long ago did the raid happen?" Marc frowned. "About half an hour," Ian replied, "but is that really important?"

"Well, it's only eleven o'clock at night," Marc retorted, "that's a departure from their usual schedule, they're stepping up their schedule. What's the rush? Why so early?" Marc reached for the telephone. "Can you put me through to Dutch intelligence?"

Marc folded up his papers. "Hello, yes, this is Marc Edwards at Scotland Yard, Major, I'm on my way to Amsterdam on a mission about *Copper Canyon*. Tell the Amsterdam armory to block off the whole armory, don't touch anything until I get there. Have a photographer standing by."

Lucerne waterfront at night

Marc looked up at Ian. "Can you get me a helicopter right away?" On the telephone again, "I want to go over the armory with a fine tooth comb – be there in about an hour."

"We're still missing something, Ian," Marc spoke up.

On the phone still again, Marc outlined his plan with Dutch Intelligence, put on his coat and disappeared out the door.

★ ★ ★

At the Dutch armory, Marc interviewed everyone involved in the theft and had a photographer take numerous pictures, even of the people being interviewed. After about two hours, he gathered up his notebook and photographs and returned to Scotland Yard with one of the Dutch military officers. They went straightaway to Marc's office and spread the pictures out on a table.

"Anybody get hurt this time?" Marc asked.

"Not seriously – the guards were tied up and chloroformed. They were knocked about a little, but not enough to get hospitalized."

Marc looked up at the officer. "How did they get in, Leftenant?"

"Well. . .through the windows first," the Dutch officer stated, "then they backed their truck up to the nearest doorway and started loading. It only took them about twenty minutes since all the alarms were disabled. There must have been a dozen thieves to load up that fast, that stuff's heavy. Any chance we can get the weapons back?"

"No, I'm afraid not, they're on their way to Venezuela already," Marc lamented. "We didn't get to the armory fast enough. Once those missiles get to Venezuela, we'll never find them – they'll get sold all over South America. BUT – Marc paused - we'll get 'em next time. Right now, let's get started putting names on these photographs."

Early the next morning, Ian appeared at Marc's office. "You look terrible. Why don't you get some sleep? Make any progress last night?"

"Quite a bit," Marc sighed out loud. "Now I know how these thefts are carried out. It's really very simple. First they study the target, maybe for a week or more. Then they cut the primary electrical lines and move in. They take out the guards, one way or another, and start loading up their transfer vehicles. Next they drive to a hidden airfield somewhere, reload onto an unregistered aircraft and off they go into the wild blue yonder. We never see them again. It all takes a minimum of time, like a commando raid, very organized."

"That's a great help, Marc," Ian commented. "Now get out of here and get some sleep before you pass out standing up."

"I need to see Erika," Marc looked up at Ian. "Meanwhile, this Dutch officer will dispense these pictures to MI6, CIA and Interpol. He also needs a ride home, he didn't get much sleep, either."

Marc drove to the Scotland Yard complex, located Erika and went to her room. "Is that bed big enough for two?" Marc smiled. "It sure is," Erika returned his smile, "but you don't look wide awake enough even to get over to it."

"You'd be amazed, just try me."

"Did you get to bed at all last night?"

"No, Ian and I spent the night looking for patterns – and we found a few."

After a long shower, Marc crawled into bed beside her. They wrapped their arms around each other and shut out the rest of the world. "I missed you so much," Marc lamented, "I could scarcely wait to get over here."

"Me too," Erika said, running her fingers through his hair. "Marc, honey, did you. . . Marc. . .Marc. . .?" His lack of response told her he was already asleep. She covered him up and headed downstairs to her office.

The next day, Ian ran into Marc's office and stood in front of him in his usual stance. Marc looked up at him and frowned.

"I know better than to ask if you have another surprise," Marc smiled, leaning back in his chair.

"Thirty minutes ago - in Paris — another armory," Ian said. They went after weapons again, AK47s, but I put the lid on it and told them to clear the area and wait for you. Can you run over there?"

"I'll need a fast ride, tell Erika so she won't worry."

In Paris, Marc repeated his Dutch investigation scheme of witnesses, pictures, and scrutiny of the crime scene. The Paris theft seemed to be accomplished in exactly the same way as the Dutch theft, and suddenly the pattern was being woven all over again. It was a breakthrough and now it all made sense. Gathering up his documents and photographs, Marc headed back to London.

"Déjà vu all over again," Marc reported, standing in Ian's office, "but now the pattern is clear. The only thing we don't have an answer for is why, why, why? What's the end product, the purpose of all this? When we learn that answer, we'll have solved the whole scheme."

Ian sat down, seemingly engrossed in his own thoughts.

"We've identified one of our agency moles," Ian mused, "a low level agent working in the archives section where he can easily get to records. He's in irons now and Scotland Yard will take care of him, but that's not to say he's the only mole. He was sloppy enough in his work to make identifying him easy, but he isn't a major player. There may be others we don't know about yet. We're making a wide sweep at both locations, here at the Yard and also at our Complex location across town. Now that we know what to look for, we'll catch others if there are any others."

"I think our Mr. Lambert has an amazingly organized force," Marc offered. "He can attack at a moment's notice with highly skilled people. Somehow he's managed to finance the entire infrastructure, probably from his thefts. It must have taken him years to slowly put all this together, demanding strict loyalty along the way, most likely by threats. And he doesn't need to warehouse his thefts; he must fence his stolen goods at the same time he attacks. That requires very close coordination.

It requires strategies as good as the D-Day Normandy invasion. In the back of my mind, I wonder that he doesn't almost have a Board of Directors with himself as the number one Chief Executive Officer. It may be just as simple as that."

Ian shifted in his chair and scratched his head. "It may be that simple, Marc, but I don't think so. What's the underlying theme? How does all this activity contribute to a single goal? What's the punch line here? If Lambert's fencing all these stolen goods, what's the overall single purpose? Granted he seems to emphasize the same subject matter over and over again. Think about it, Marc; top of the line artworks – weapons, always the same objects, automatic rifles and handguns – and we know he's an expert at kidnapping women for sexual slavery – smaller art objects such as manuscripts and church objects. Is he just building a huge bank account? But for what reason?"

"Well, we know that occasionally he does something just for a show of power," Marc said, "but that's just plain ego. He's displaying his ability to steal and get away with it. His ego must be as big as the Atlantic Ocean; he's laughing at us. But why, because everything still fits all together. What's his single, overriding purpose?"

Marc slapped his knee. "He can't be just a collector or he'd have a warehouse somewhere as big as Piccadilly Circus. None of our investigations have discovered a warehouse – or maybe we haven't even been looking for one?"

Ian stood up and walked to the window. He was greeted by a day filled with sunshine and an endless blue sky. People scampered all across Trafalgar Square, in and out of stores and eating places, everyone on a personal, private mission of some kind. This one single elusive piece to the Lambert puzzle was terribly worrisome.

Marc began pacing the floor along with Ian. "Does he have some kind of schedule? I don't think so, he seems to be taking his own time with everything – the thefts, the attacks on us and on Erika. . .except his murders," Marc suddenly blurted out. "Every time we capture one of his henchmen, he kills him immediately. There's no waiting around. He doesn't want us to get any information about his plans or his organization. He's jealously guarding those secrets. Why?"

Ian finally turned toward Marc. "Why don't you bring Erika up to date on where we stand at the moment, and listen to her thinking out loud. I'll bet she might have some interesting insights into all this. Why don't you give it a try? We can set up a confidential War Room downstairs just like they did during World War II so we can iron out the details. By the way, where did she get all her training to be able to build a professional viewpoint on all this?"

"She's a university girl, Ian," Marc said. "Her everyday job was a Chief Computer Programmer for a company with a number of branches around the U.S. She's able to multi-task with a dozen or more locations at the same time, and she can think pretty fast. She's very good at what she does, especially with organizational matters, which makes her highly useful at these kinds of tasks. We probably should have put her to work a long time ago, although her mind-set right now is on her own survival. She'll come around, let's give her a meaningful role in the scheme of things and she'll meet the challenge."

"Very good," Ian said, "sit with her and explain everything we know about this gang of thieves. Then we'll pick her brain."

When Marc explained the need for her opinion, Erika became excited and was ready to put her mind at work thinking about the multitude of events that had been happening. At last she was going to be really helpful toward solving this strange enigma.

"I'll do whatever I can, Marc, but just remember, I don't really think the way you police people do. You're all very fact-oriented and logical, and you know how to pick an event apart."

"Yes, but you're very logical in your thinking, too," Marc answered. "No one is more logical and fact-oriented than a computer guru with your kind of experience. All you have to do is switch your orientation from computers to police work. You know by now how we operate, how we string facts together into very logical orientations. We're dealing with people, and that means people are often very illogical, even confused because people become emotional and they run off-track because they're angry or in love or sometimes just stupid. Human emotion gets in the way of logical thinking. That should make sense to you. It's all the same, maybe just different a little."

"Okay, let's get started, Mr. Psychologist," she waved her hand.

"Not quite yet," Marc chimed in, "we need to sit in a sound proof room for a few hours and talk about details; maybe we can slip up to your room afterward."

For two hours over coffee and tea, Erika and Marc discussed the entire dilemma of the gang and its activities, focusing on details about its operation and the precision in which it carries out the strikes. There were a number of highly important choke points that needed discussing. They talked about manpower requirements, methods of transportation, use of various tools, methods of researching their targets, warehousing, lines of communication, history of specific strikes, and much more. Erika called for a computer and they prepared an executive summary type of written document. Then the two of them called for Ian.

After another hour or so of discussion, they arrived at a preliminary plan of execution involving the total group of law enforcement agencies. Ian took over control of *Operation Lady Luck*, calling for another immediate all-agency conference in London in two days, including the French, British MI6, Interpol, and the American CIA.

Marc and Erika slipped away for two days to take a tour of the London sights and English countryside, and to mentally unwind by taking their minds off their work. By clearing their minds, however, they were totally unprepared for the attack that was being mounted against them at the Stonehenge monument on Salisbury Plain.

Medieval Watch Tower, Lucerne, Switzerland

"What an amazing piece of architecture, Marc," Erika shook her head. "It will take centuries to figure out how it was actually built, won't it?"

"That's the easy part," Marc chuckled. "Imagine the ingenuity of having to physically prove all those theories, right or wrong," he added as they climbed into their car, "to say nothing about how they moved those monstrous stones."

Marc put the key in the ignition and turned it to start the engine. There was a slow groaning noise as the engine tried to start up. It was not the first time Marc had heard the same sound. He immediately turned off the key and shouted out loud.

"Out. . .out, Erika. .," Marc screamed as loud as he could, "fast, hurry, don't look back, just run as hard as you can." They both made about fifty feet or so before the car erupted with a horrendous explosion, spewing billows of black smoke and red-orange flames. They both were thrown flat on the ground when the car exploded a second time.

Concussions from the sheer magnitude of the detonations took a sudden and heavy toll on their bodies. Erika's outer clothes were sheared off her body and she lay on the ground in her underwear. Shrapnel from the exploding car cut into her arms and legs and at the same time blew her shoes away. Marc's shirt sleeves were stripped from his arms and his pants legs were shredded.

Erika and Marc were unconscious when medical help arrived at the grim scene. Put into two separate ambulances, they were rushed to a London hospital in critical condition. Three tourists were killed in the parking lot along with the destruction of several nearby vehicles. The next day, both were in treatment in the same room and slowly beginning to recuperate, and they were in a state of confusion.

"They tell me you're a hard pair to kill," the doctor smiled slightly. "I guess you know you're lucky to be alive. Twenty feet closer to your car and we'd be picking you up with a wet towel. There's someone here to see you already."

Marc looked up and recognized Ian standing beside his bed. "Hi, Ian, we ran into a small problem out at Stonehenge."

"What is it with you two," Ian grumbled, "we can't seem to let you out alone, you just keep getting into trouble over and over again."

"Somebody out there doesn't like us, I guess," Erika tried to smile. "I lost my wig, I don't have any hair at all, and I have a broken arm. Does this mean I get to take a vacation?"

"Always trying to get out of work," Marc bantered.

"You two may be a little banged up," Ian commented, "but that doesn't mean you're going to get out of attending the conference Thursday. You still have another whole day to get back on your feet."

"You really have a great heart, mother, I'll remember you in my will," Marc stared at Ian and made a face at him.

Pointing at Erika, the doctor said, "This one has a broken arm, and that one over there has a broken leg. You have a tough company to work for," the doctor smiled.

"When you both are ready to leave," Ian reminded, "let me know and I'll send a limo for you. Remember, though, a few broken bones shouldn't keep your heads from working. Make certain you're at that conference, crutches or not. We need your thoughts on just about everything, this whole matter is extremely important."

The conference room on Thursday was filled to capacity with high level law enforcement representatives from all over Europe and North America. Ian took a deep breath and walked over to the podium.

"I'm pleased to tell you," Ian began, "that we finally have some critical breakthroughs, thanks to these twoYankee ruffians who were attacked two nights ago and barely escaped with their lives." He pointed at Erika and Marc. "The document you're holding is an Executive Summary report of the life and activities of the *Operation Lady Luck* group. It's an exhaustive report of six pages, based on our most recent thinking.

I'm sorry I can't wait for you to read all six pages right at the moment, but based on this report we're going to devise a trap that should net us the entire organization – except for Mr. Lambert. So far, we have no idea who he is, except his real name is NOT Mr. Lambert, and we don't know his nationality. MI6, Interpol and the American CIA have positive proof that "Philip George Lambert" is buried in a cemetery in Cologne, Germany after having died of a stroke four years ago. Interpol even had the body exhumed to make sure there actually was a body buried there.

My Deputy, Derek Childers, was killed in the same attack that went after Lieutenant Edwards and Erika Stevens. Scotland Yard is now on the point in this offensive and I'm at the fine edge of that point. All communication will be handled through my office, with the help of Miss Stevens. Communications Office will be here at Scotland Yard and we will coordinate all incoming intel. My Deputy Chief Inspector replacing Childers is now James Barker (stand up, Jim, so they can get a look at you), a veteran Inspector of fifteen years who also will handle incoming communications.

Director of Field Operations is now Harold Roberts (stand up, Harry) who will coordinate all field operations including joint attacks by law enforcement. Our task is to monitor all *Operation Lady Luck* activities and past attacks, prepare a massive simultaneous final attack, and activate that attack at the same moment all across Europe in about nine or ten cities. All arrests will require incarceration at single sites including immediate interrogation of captors. The Prime Minister has directed that during our attacks, we are permitted extreme force if necessary — shoot to kill, gentlemen, our enemies will do the same.

This huge gang of thieves operates as a large corporation, most likely with a Board of Directors and a CEO who may or may not be Mr. Lambert. It may even have connections with the Mafia, and certainly is connected to local gangs and local gang leaders. Probably the Mafia is scared to death of this outfit. If the truth was known, they may even have a finance department like Al Capone did in Chicago. It's easy to hire criminal help on a budget the way Lambert operates.

For our purposes, communication will be paramount — if in doubt, communicate! For you in this room right now, you should know that this room will be made into a War Room with computers and telephones. We'll be ready for you when you're organized and begin sending your reports. Now, here's how the **simultaneous offensive** will take place:

> *One*: a period of **monitoring** the thieves will not exceed a period of two weeks. Get close in on the enemy, use stakeouts to watch for Lambert's employees and eventually put them in handcuffs. This period will begin August 1 and end on August 14

> *Two*: you will undergo **preparation for attack** for seven days following – ending August 21. All attack plans must be filed with me by August 21

> *Three*: individually, **attacks will take place** three days following the twenty-first using local law enforcement and whatever resources are necessary. Attack time will be 0200 hours Greenwich Mean Time

Four: **attacks on strongholds** will require immediate lockdowns; **single attacks** will require immediate arrest and incarceration; arrests will require total inability of combatants to communicate among themselves or with the world outside the jails; please prepare your jailers accordingly. NEVER put those you arrest together in the same jail cell. Keep them from communicating with each other.

Five: if you **capture people** who seem to be in some kind of **command authority**, suggesting they might hold an executive type of position, <u>they will remain in handcuffs *and* leg chains even when jailed</u>, and we need to know who they are. Tell me immediately and I'll send an interrogation specialist to your location.

We're going to recess now for forty-five minutes so you'll have time to read over the report and prepare questions. To save time, please write out your questions before we gather this afternoon. We'll come together again at 11:15 and end the conference as close to noon as possible. Lunch is on us again, gentlemen. And whatever you do, don't show your document to ANYONE, not even your most trusted associates. This is a plan requiring *zero failure*.

Immediately the room became a beehive of voices. Erika reached across the table and squeezed Marc's hand. "This is very exciting, Marc," she said smiling, "we have a mighty force on our side, don't we?"

"Probably a force of up to four thousand law enforcement," Marc countered, "when you count local police departments all across Europe and North America. No doubt this is the largest police net in history - and the most dedicated. Remember, this gang of thieves has hit every European nation, and each nation wants its own revenge. We have two and a half days to ourselves, hon, what would you like to do in those two days?"

"Let's go to the Yard Complex first," she suggested. "This entire offensive could get to be dangerous – and very busy. You'll eventually have to be here at the Yard, won't you?"

Marc heaved a sign of concern. "Yes, but you don't have to be here. Maybe you'd better stay at the Compound."

"Oh no you don't," she shot back, "after what we've been through, I want a seat on the fifty yard line. You'll need some help, so I want to be sitting right beside you."

Ian fought his way through the crowd to get to Marc and Erika. "The two of you have forty eight hours to yourselves, let the Yard get set up while you take some days off. Then we're going to need you at a desk, especially Erika. You're both going to be absolutely invaluable. For now, go ahead and disappear for a while."

"That's perfect planning, Ian," Marc agreed, "we need a little time to get ourselves ready. See you then."

At the compound and alone at last, they melted into each other's arms. "I love you, Erika, so very much," he said as he caressed her head and gave her a few long kisses. "Maybe when this is all over we can take some time at Tenby and just relax."

"I've never had a real boyfriend," she held him close, "certainly not someone I really care for as much as I love you. This whole affair could get pretty ugly, but I want to give myself to you before it all starts. We've been lucky so far – escaped some really bad times – but I wonder what's about to happen to us now."

With that said, they took the telephone off the hook and turned the lights off. The massive attack by *Operation Lady Luck* could go either way. Maybe just before the attacks begin would be the last time they could be alone for quite a while, and they made the most of it. Now there was no doubt for either of them; they loved each other without a doubt. If they could both survive the coming difficult period, they could begin making plans for their future.

Night scene Lucerne waterfront

7

In the dead quiet of early morning, all across Europe and North America, the attack pressed forward. In Edinburgh, London, Paris, Marseilles, Berlin, Munich, Vienna, Amsterdam, Lucerne, Berne, even Barcelona and Dublin, thousands of law enforcement officers spread the tightest single police net ever put into motion. In terms of arrests, the numbers became staggering. Law officers cleared the streets of known criminals and of other thugs suspected of affiliations with the Lambert gang.

Marc's telephone rang. "Hello, this is Lieutenant Marc Edwards, send your message."

"This is Interpol Paris office of *Operation Lady Luck*. We have a suspect in custody that we believe could be a high-level gang member. He's a little more educated than most of these blokes. How do you want us to proceed with him?"

"Put him in a single cell with handcuffs *and* leg chains. Ask him does he know Mr. Lambert or if he is in fact Mr. Lambert. If he goes berserk, turns white faced, or begins to twitch in his chair, call me back immediately." Marc hung up and waited for the next call, which came right away.

"Hello, this is Lieutenant Marc Edwards, what is your message?"

"This is the Paris Interpol office again. We have a second suspect, a good candidate for the top of the food chain. This ruffian is clean-shaven and a bit belligerent. We had to restrain him but he's in a cell with cuffs on at both ends. What do you want us to do with him?"

"I'll tell you the same thing I told the other officer," Mark reiterated, "put him in a single cell, don't take off his handcuffs or leg irons, and ask him if he is Mr. Lambert or if he knows where Lambert is. If he suddenly gets extremely quiet, won't talk and looks really scared when you mention Lambert's name, call me back and we'll discuss him." The voice said okay and started to hang up the phone.

"Wait a minute," Marc quickly added, "what about casualties? Did you lose any officers?"

"Only one," the voice answered, "these hoods came along easily."

"Our attack has just started and you've already had two calls from Interpol," Erika recalled, "we're going to have a busy night."

"Erika, it's time to sharpen the knife," Marc said standing up. "I have to go to Paris and talk to these two birds. I'll be back tomorrow, honey, take my messages for me." He shuffled off with help from a crutch.

Erika looked up at him. "Please be careful, Marc, we've stirred up the pot and everything's in motion. Don't get shot at, honey. I'll worry about you 'til I see you here again," she called after him.

By helicopter, Paris was only forty-five minutes away. Marc rushed into the Interpol office and went right away to the interrogation section. "Okay, where are these two clowns?" he asked.

"Over in the back, in the holding tanks," an officer directed him. In a short time, he was seated across the table from the first suspect who simply slouched in his chair and stared at Marc who sat quietly reading over the custody papers. Finally closing up the file and looking across at his subject, Marc managed to force himself to yawn.

"I see here you're listed as Pierre Camille," he began. "Is that your real name?" There was no response from the suspect. Marc let more time pass in silence. "You're in a pile of trouble, buddy. How did you get mixed up with this rowdy bunch?"

More time went by in silence as the two men stared at each other. A little later, Marc stood up and rounded the corner of the table to sit on its edge. He leaned slightly toward the suspect and calmly began to read from the arrest file.

"Conspiracy to commit murder, accessory to murder, resisting arrest, grand theft, marketing illegal weapons, marketing cocaine, assault on a police officer. . .that's good for about life in prison," Marc read the charges. "You'll never see the light of day, Mr. Pierre Camille. How do you plead to these charges?"

Pierre looked at Marc. "I'll be out of here in twenty-four hours," Pierre sneered. Marc smiled back at him.

"Think Lambert's going to get you out? Not a chance, Lambert's in the cell next to yours getting ready for the hangman. You better save yourself, Lambert can't do anything for you."

"Lambert can do anything, he's too powerful even for you, I'm not worried," Pierre laughed.

"Well, your Mr. Lambert says he doesn't even know you."

"We'll see about that," Pierre said.

"What's Lambert's real name? Where does he live? How soon will he send someone to eliminate you?"

"I'm too valuable to eliminate," Pierre replied.

"That's what the last executive said; now he's put away in a pine box. Don't kid yourself, Pierre, everybody is expendable including you. It's easy to train somebody to take your place. He's already planning how to kill you."

"No, not true," Pierre jumped up from his chair. "He wouldn't do that." Marc knew he was getting through to the man finally, so he switched tactics.

"The people who arrested you aren't bound by legal ethics," Marc started off. "They'll put you through the wringer just like your organization does to your victims. You know how brutal Mr. Lambert is – he'll stop at nothing to get what he wants, including torture. What's a little torture between friends, nobody will know about it anyway. Lambert sits in his tiny little office making phone calls and punching a computer while you take all the risks. It's always the same old story."

"His office isn't tiny, it's huge," Pierre boasted, "and it sits high up so he has a global view of the world. You have no idea how powerful he is. One word from him and governments fall."

"I don't think so," Marc snickered, "his office is like all the others, a basement throw-together that doesn't even have windows in it because the boss is hiding from the rest of the world."

"Oh no, he built his stronghold on a mount. . ." Suddenly Pierre stopped, realizing he had just given away an important secret. He sat down and didn't speak another word. The interrogation was over, and Mark had another secret to add to all the others. Pierre had just egotistically boasted himself into a corner.

Marc left the room in search of the second suspect. This time he sat in an interrogation room across the table from Marcel Dufrey, a somewhat well-dressed man, in his fifties most likely, bald with a moustache. The sun had been up for hours and Marc was starting to tire, but he needed to grill the man.

"Marcel Dufrey from Paris," Marc began, "let's see what kind of trouble you've got yourself into. Conspiracy to commit murder, accessory to murder, resisting arrest, grand theft, marketing illegal weapons, marketing cocaine, assault on a police officer. . .that's good for about life in prison," Marc read the charges.

"You'll never prove any of that," the man became arrogant, "you don't even have enough to hold me on. I'll be out of here in a matter of hours," he boasted.

"That's just a start, there are a number of other charges, too," Marc reminded. "You'll never see the streets again, that's for sure. Lambert's not going to waste any time springing you, you're just a part time employee, not even high enough on the organization chart to be a thought in his head." Marc waited for the bait to sink in.

"You fool," Dufrey spouted, "you don't know what you're dealing with. Lambert will have me out of here in minutes."

"You've already been in here for four hours, Lambert must be dragging his feet on you, if there really is a Lambert somewhere. Lambert's probably the cleaning man who goes around cleaning offices for a living. So what are you going to plead, guilty or not guilty?"

"Lambert is the most powerful man in the world," Dufrey boasted. "From his mountain top compound, he controls the infrastructure of most governments. When he reaches his goal, governments will fall, believe me. Even America isn't safe from his grand plan, but you'll be dead by then along with that stupid bitch you've been screwing every night."

Marc's head jerked up away from the arrest documents. "Now, now," Marc chided him, "let's not get nasty now. Lambert doesn't even know about me, he's not that smart. Everything always looks good on paper, but down in his basement hideaway he calls an office, he thinks he can control everything. Too bad his secret plan will never hatch, but that's the way it is with third class citizens.

"I've seen his grand plan, and I've seen it at work," Dufrey was on his feet. "All he has to do is make a few clicks on his computer and things automatically happen. You'll see pretty soon."

"Look at this sketch," Marc goaded, "Lambert's an old man and he hasn't even started on his great plan. Somebody's got you fooled, although I doubt there even is a Mr. Lambert."

"There is, all right, and he's seen you and the bitch both. I don't know how you got out of that car crash. He'll be after you again before you know it, and next time he won't miss."

"Here's a question for you," Marc spoke up. "What's 73 plus 29 plus 92?"

"What's that supposed to mean?" Dufrey sneered.

"Quick, what's the answer?" Marc pushed onward.

"194, anyone knows that, but it doesn't mean anything. It's just a number."

Marc packed up his papers and left the room, deciding Dufrey most likely had something to do with finances. The man was a gold mine of information. His ego and his arrogance gave away the entire Lambert situation. Marc was positive the name Lambert was an alias. But it still didn't point the way to his real name. Within the hour, Marc was back at Scotland Yard by mid-afternoon, working on profiling Lambert. Erika was happy to see him back and threw her arms around his neck. "Thank heaven you're back in one piece," she squealed, "I prayed for you while you were gone. Did you get what you went for?"

"That and much more – I really hit pay dirt. Can you take my calls while I work on this profile?" She gladly agreed, while he slaved over the pile of papers in front of him. For two hours he worked on the profile, merging together as much of the separate pieces of information as he could gather. Finally he returned to where Erika was seated at the bank of computers.

"Where did you learn how to profile?" she quizzed him.

"It was part of my FBI training, I just hope I'm up to it," Marc replied.

Marc continued to merge all the pieces of information he had, putting them into one presentable review. The seemingly unrelated statements from various individuals he had interviewed all came together into one document that the FBI termed a "Suspect Profile". Calling for Ian, they both put the document in proper shape, then passed it to one of the visiting FBI agents who said it was ready for dissemination. Going over to the War Room loudspeaker, Marc called for everyone's attention and stepped up to the podium.

"Listen up, please, I'm passing out a document known as a 'Suspect Profile', based on the most recent information we have. Please read it carefully again the moment you get it. We've spent a good deal of time preparing this document, and if you want to understand this man Lambert, now is your chance." Marc began to read from the document.

Subject Profile: Mr. Lambert
Author: Lieutenant Marcus Edwards, Manchester, Missouri Police Department, USA

The Mastermind antagonist behind the global attacks and thefts has the name Philip George Lambert, an alias. We don't yet know his real name but we're getting closer to the truth.

Psychological Evaluation
A highly intelligent individual of exceptional organizational skills with a simultaneous global outreach. He can direct multiple geographic activities of his organization with an uncanny time-sensitive precision. IQ estimates put him in the top one percent of the global population, at about 200+.

(Lambert) directs the activities of his organization much like the Chief Executive Officer of a corporation, with several lieutenants who contribute their talents to the ongoing success of the organization.

(Lambert) has a huge ego and an equally huge pride, so much so that he believes he cannot be stopped by conventional law enforcement means. He can be very ruthless, resorting to torture and/ or killing as methods of revenge or control of his immediate staff. Although no one has given him a psychological assessment, he appears to have a mega-maniac personality coupled with a large anger reservoir that occasionally presents itself with explosive violence. He can't be pushed into an activity that he cannot control, but if cornered gives vent to his highly explosive anger. His superior intellect prevents him from seeking or receiving suggestions or ideas that are not his own, possibly hindering activities somewhat.

Major Activities

(Lambert) conducts thefts ranging from drugs, works of art, jewelry and weapons to assassinations and female abductions for sex slave trafficking. Such activities are timed precisely, sometimes several at one time. His employees usually are out-sourced locally and are well paid. Objects of thefts are transported immediately, usually within a few hours. There is no evidence of warehouse activities. Guards who protected these objects are either killed outright or chloroformed. Activities are conducted almost entirely under cover of darkness; his plans are always successful and are conducted with the meticulous planning that has become his trademark. He is assisted by a small group of educated criminals who are fiercely loyal to him and are accustomed to always being successful in their own endeavors.

End of Report

Marc returned to his seat and breathed a sigh of relief. He felt the document was very accurate and would serve as a focal point for all law enforcement agencies. At that moment, an orderly came over to him advising that an urgent phone call had just come in for him.

"Hello Marc, this is your Interpol liaison. With apologies, it is my duty to tell you that both Pierre Camille and Marcel Dufrey have been helped to escape from Interpol custody and are now at large. One guard was killed outright and another chloroformed. It was a lightning quick escape, no doubt masterminded by Lambert. We had them under close watch and we have agents scouring the countryside without any luck yet."

Marc banged his fist on the table and swore out loud. "How the hell did he manage that without getting caught? I bet the jailers forgot to put leg chains on either of them. We just lost our two best witnesses."

"Oh, I forgot to tell you," Erika spoke up, "someone has been trying to hack into our computer systems again. I don't think they've quite managed to get through yet, but they're trying hard enough. I've used three computer guard programs, but it may only be a matter of time until they're successful."

"Keep trying, Erika, we need more time. We can't seem to catch up to where we want to be, there are too many distractions."

Marc's telephone rang again and, reluctantly, he picked up the receiver. "Marc Edwards here."

"This is the Interpol Administration and Research Office at Lyon. I have some interesting news for you, Marc. I uncovered some old documents prepared after the Nuremberg Trials. I found the documents while I was rummaging through some old files. We've managed to find out Lambert's real name, and you're going to be quite surprised."

Marc sat up straight in his chair. "Amazing, tell me about it."

"His real name is Gustav Blaatner, son of Dr. Rudolph Blaatner, hanged for war crimes after the Nuremberg Trials. There's almost nothing about him during his very early years, but his name popped up as having received his medical degree from the Berlin Medical Institute in the American sector of Germany. Prior to that, he attended lower school where he graduated first in his class with a remarkable record of academic achievement that brought him an invitation to attend medical school on a four-year grant, all expenses paid.

His mother is listed as Gertrude Schultz, deceased by suicide, but she never married his father. Her suicide took place several weeks after the father was executed. So he didn't know either of his parents, a problem that evidently warped his emotions pretty badly since both his parents died by hanging.

Anyway, Lambert is actually Dr. Gustav Blaatner. He stayed on three years at the Institute in a teaching position, then several more as a consultant. Again he attained an amazing academic record. After that he kind of disappeared and there's no record of him any longer except for a notation by the Politzei Berliner that he was questioned about the murder of several young women in Berlin. Probably would have lost contact with him but the murders were pretty bizarre.

There were three women; the external sex organs of all three of them were precisely and surgically removed after they were killed by forced alcohol ingestion and strangulation. That had to have been done by a medical expert, but the police couldn't prove enough to charge him and they had to turn him loose. So, I thought you would like to know the details; these facts explain a great deal about his behavior as an adult – and as a psychopath with some strange kind of sociopathic tendencies. You might want to be careful, he's most likely capable, literally, of any kind of criminal behavior."

"I certainly am indebted to you for passing the information on to me," Marc thanked the man. "Our own researchers had to give up the chase when they couldn't turn up anything, so this is definitely a major, major breakthrough for us. If you learn anything more, please give me a ring. I'm certainly in your debt because this profile answers quite a few nagging questions for which we had no answers at all."

"Well, actually, there is one more thing I forgot to mention, but I'm not certain it will tie into the Blaatner background. Gustav was found guilty of another string of murders – women again, but he escaped from the jail he was held in. This time the women were members of the jury that convicted him and they ranged in age from thirty-two to forty-seven. Blaatner killed the women with an ice pick in the neck and their bodies again were pretty badly mutilated. The medical examiner that conducted the autopsies found the women's blood alcohol was six times the limit required for intoxication.

The trial was held in Vienna and it received a lot of publicity and the newspapers carried the story blow by blow for more than two weeks. I have a cousin working for the Vienna newspaper that ran the story and I asked him to look up the daily installments. One fact that never was given to the newspapers was that Blaatner was recaptured and sent to the Vienna Institute for Health Rehabilitation in Vienna. It's a mental institution. He escaped again after only six months and was never heard from after that."

"You're a genius and I'm completely in your debt," Marc finished up. Then he turned to Erika. "Another piece to the puzzle, Erika, Interpol just told me that Lambert's real name is Gustav Blaatner, or rather DOCTOR Gustav Blaatner. So now we know at last. The enigma is slowly unraveling, thank heaven. Lambert graduated from medical school, which gives him access to as many women as he wants to carve up. I'll write a report as soon as I can. Now Gustav has a complete outlet to his psychopathology. He can kill as many women as he feels like, and carve them up any way he wishes."

"Marc, there's an American colonel in uniform asking to see you," another orderly stood by Marc's desk.

"Wonderful, let's hope he has some good news too, show him in, we certainly could use more good news today."

"Hello, Marc," the Colonel said, "I'm Colonel Ted Richards from the American 82nd Airborne Division, a special company of Rangers and Seals assigned to the British 6th Airborne Division for mountain training. I need to talk to you in private, rather quickly."

"No such thing in this room, Colonel," Marc retorted. "This is Erika Stevens, a computer expert, and the guy over there is Chief Inspector Ian Brooks of Scotland Yard. You can speak freely in front of them."

Marc called Ian over and explained the Colonel's presence. "We can go into a sound proof room if you think it's necessary," Marc added.

"Yes, by all means, *it is necessary*," and they moved to the new location.

"Colonel, I hate to do this to you, but I'm going to need some identification, some proof of who you are," Marc said.

"That's easy enough, and I don't blame you." He pulled out his ID cards and showed them around.

"What can we do for you, Colonel?" Ian prompted, "we're in the middle of a critical situation right now."

"It's rather what we can do for you," the Colonel said. "You aren't aware of it, but the CIA has been working closely with the

FBI tracking this entire scenario; they know you just lost two of your best witnesses. The best part is that the CIA knows where they are right now and will continue monitoring them. Even better, it seems your two witnesses have teamed up with two more high echelon characters and they're all in the same place in a safe house of their own. How would you like to catch them all at one time?"

"Would I, this is fantastic!" Ian blurted out, jumping to his feet. "Can you really do that? Who's the CIA man?"

"Of course he won't reveal his identity, but he's genuine enough, I'll vouch for that. The CIA's been aware of the gang for about a year and has been doing its homework."

Marc squinted at the Colonel momentarily, then carefully asked the question. "How do we go about this, Colonel, what do you propose?"

"From our standpoint, it's relatively easy," the Colonel said, "just a matter of split-second timing. We'll storm the safe house, grab the four bastards and kill the rest if we have to. We also can take them to a special place where you can interrogate them thoroughly. All you have to do is come along and ID the idiots, and go with us to the interrogation rooms. Or, you can do your own interrogation, whichever you prefer, but you'll have to do it at a location of our choice."

"How long are the bastards going to be at that safe house?" Ian asked.

"We don't know, they could leave at any time since they all just came together. If they leave, we'll tail along with them. They'll most likely stay there until they think it's safe to move. Right now they're playing it safe – probably two to three days more, max."

"Let's move on it," Marc decided, "we need to put them through the ringer. We need some really important answers about their leader, and we need those answers now."

"Our team's waiting and ready to go," the Colonel said, "and they've been briefed on what's to be done. Let's get moving."

"I want to go," Erika spoke up, "I have a vested interest in this."

"Two reasons why you can't go," Marc spun around. "First, if there's shooting you could easily get shot or killed. Second reason, you need to keep those hackers off our back. Please, honey, stay out of this one, you've already had four or five close calls."

"I'm disappointed, Marc, but I won't push it. I guess you have your mind made up, anyway."

"You can watch the raid on the TV monitor, we'll have a camera with us," he added, then he leaned over and kissed her.

"Don't I get a kiss, too?" Ian pouted playfully.

"Get out of here you naughty little boy," Erika played along, "your wife wouldn't approve."

The fully outfitted attack squad of eight specialists took up their positions at the front and back doors of the safe house outside Paris. Ian and Marc drew their guns and waited. At a signal, the squad leader broke through the front door, his lighted pistol at the ready. Inside, the gang members jumped to their feet.

"Police, police, on the floor with your hands on your heads, now–now–now, move, get down," the Colonel shouted.

The squad rushed in and went through each room. Altogether there were seven gang members and three half-dressed young girls who screamed at the abrupt confusion, trying to cover themselves. The other part of the attack squad burst in from the back door, shouting. It was confusing, but luckily there was no shooting until one of the gang drew his gun and fired at a soldier who returned fire and killed him. It was all over in a few minutes. Bound and handcuffed, the gang was led out of the house and put into a military van; the girls were put out on the street and told to leave.

At the military compound, each prisoner was placed in a separate cell so the group couldn't talk among themselves. Cameras were set up in the hallways and military guards were told to keep the prisoners quiet. The high echelon prisoners were tagged for first interrogation.

Outside the building, a chest-high barrier circled the premises along with more military guards wearing flak jackets, two tanks and several armored vehicles. Three snipers perched on top the buildings. All outside military guards were ordered to shoot anyone who approached the doors to the building, no matter who they were.

Marc sat in the interrogation room waiting for Marcel Dufrey who finally was led into the room clad only in his underwear. Ian and the Colonel stood behind the two-way mirror to watch the proceedings.

"Well, well, Dufrey, so we meet again," Marc said cheerfully. "Have a seat and we'll chat a while. Looks like you didn't get very far, did you? We have a lot to talk about, neighbor, shall we get started? By the way, there's no sign of Mr. Lambert, fella, so I guess you've been thrown to the wolves."

Marc's greeting was followed by complete silence. He waited some fifteen minutes reading over some documents before moving a muscle, then pushed a sheet of paper over in front of Dufrey that outlined the charges against him along with individual prescribed sentences of incarceration. Dufrey was unable to control his emotions when he read the pronouncements. His eyes blinked repeatedly and he shifted continually in his chair. Marc said nothing.

Finally the prisoner slammed his hand flat on the table. "I want to see legal counsel," he said, trying to keep his voice as evenly toned as possible. More time passed in silence. Dufrey spoke out again. "I want to see a barrister!" he said more loudly this time.

"I'm afraid there's no legal help available just now," Marc answered, "You're entirely on your own, old man. In fact there isn't another soul within five miles. You see, I'm working outside the law just as you did. I could torture the hell out of you and no one would even know it – and I just might do that if I get impatient with you."

"You can't do that, it's illegal," Dufrey erupted, "I have rights."

"Not in this building, not today," Marc smiled. "You see, we're going to play this exactly how you boys operate. I offer you no quarter, Dufrey, and I have *carte blanc* to treat you any way I wish. So let's stop fooling around. You've been had, old chum, and you'd better tell us everything you know if you don't want to go out of here in a body bag. Either way, walking upright or in a body bag, it makes no difference to me. I don't care if you're alive or dead."

Dufrey stood up and walked back and forth, shoving his hands in his pockets. Marc kept silent, waiting for the man's anxiety to force him into breaking down. After some time, Dufrey sat down resolutely. He sensed Marc meant what he said. "What do you want to know?"

"Who is Mr. Lambert?"

Dufrey's face paled and he started to whimper. After a few moments, he started to talk in a soft voice.

"Nobody knows, except Lambert isn't his real name." Marc pushed the sketch over in front of him. "Is this a reasonable likeness of him?"

Dufrey studied the sketch and finally spoke up. "Yeah, except he's a bit thinner than this, a few inches less than six feet tall and about 175 pounds. He's not British, you know." Marc ignored the comment.

"Where's his hideout?" Marc pushed on.

"He has two - I've only seen one of them, both supposedly close to Lucerne, Switzerland. They say his primary stronghold is on top of a mountain somewhere, but nobody can say for sure. There's a lesser one on land level. He never meets with us on his mountaintop, just at the lower level where he has his office staff. Supposedly the lower office is fixed with explosives so he can destroy it at the push of a button. It's in a hotel."

"You think he'd kill his office staff if he thought it necessary?" Marc asked.

Dufrey snorted. "He'd sacrifice anybody, he's a maniac. I've seen him kill one of his Directors in the blink of an eye. He's merciless. He won't try to save us now, he'll try to kill us before we can talk. I'm surprised he hasn't tried already. Either way, I'm a dead man; it's the gallows or assassination."

Marc looked up at him. "I'll see what I can do with your sentencing for cooperating with us, but I can't promise anything. It all depends on who the magistrate is. Will you fill us in on his global contacts – Paris, Munich, Vienna, Amsterdam, Edinburgh and so on?"

"If you'll try to reduce my sentence," Dufrey pleaded, "I could be very grateful, I don't want to die at the end of a needle."

"I said I'll do the best I can," Marc promised as he called for a stenographer. "Give this lady as much information as you can, then we'll talk again."

"Lieutenant, Lieutenant," one of the guards grabbed Marc by the shoulder. "You gotta come in here. I think one of these low lifes has something to tell you. It must be important, he's pretty worked up over it."

Marc went into another holding cell. "What's on your mind, buddy?" Marc looked across the room at him.

"I want to make a deal," the man said. "I know where all the art works are, I can take you right to them, but I'll only trade 'em for a reduced sentence. What do you say?"

Marc and the man talked at length until they understood each other. Suddenly all the information Marc was receiving seemed to center around Switzerland and Marc pulled Ian aside.

"Ian, everything I'm hearing points to Switzerland," Marc said, "what do you think? Could that be where Lambert's stronghold is located? The guy I just talked to says he knows where all the artwork can be found. Maybe Lambert is warehousing the art; he can get quick cash for guns and drugs, even the women he's kidnapped, but paintings are different."

Ian let his breath out and flopped into a chair. "Well that seems logical, but then why is he stealing paintings if he doesn't market them quickly? You think it's just to convince everyone of his power? If Lambert is just stockpiling art, what's the point? Why even bother?"

Marc scratched his growing beard and looked at the wall. "That's the only explanation that makes any sense. Why don't we meet this bum's offer and let him show us where the stash is hidden?"

"I'll go along with that," Ian decided. "I'll set up the trip to Lucerne for tomorrow noon, but if he's just playing us, I'll lock him up and throw the key away."

In mid-afternoon, their plane from London landed at a pre-arranged destination and they transferred to a bus for the ride to Lucerne. The Fall season was about to descend on the broad sweeping slopes of the Swiss Alps. The temperature was predicted to begin its annual drop in another month, but for now a brilliant sunshine bathed the naked summertime peaks and valleys with an enchanting, kaleidoscopic wash of rainbow colors. The bus strained to wind in and out of the jagged landscape, twisting and turning in sometimes-dangerous hairpin whips. At last the twinkling lights of the beautiful city of Lucerne lay spread out before them at the foot of some of the taller rises of the world-renowned Swiss Alps.

"Okay, tour leader, where do we go from here?" Marc questioned Lambert's henchman.

"The warehouse is hidden because of its dilapidated condition," the shackled man explained. "You'd think it was ready to be torn down. The windows and doors are boarded up to keep people out.

The walls have been sprayed with dust and colored brick-dirt. But the inside is surprising. . . you'll see."

The bus drew up to a worn out building and stopped. True to the man's description, the building appeared to be on the verge of collapse. They all piled out of the bus and followed the leader to a side door, camouflaged to look like a simple rock wall. The man fumbled with a hidden switch and a doorway slid open. Inside, spotlights bathed the interior in a warm glow. The transformation to an ultra-modern art gallery seemed magical and Marc suddenly drew in his breath in amazement. He couldn't believe what he was seeing. The room was filled with some of the world's most spectacular works of art, and for a few solitary moments the group stood motionless in awe.

"I can't believe what I'm seeing," Marc gasped, turning to Ian. "Look at this! Here's a Monet and a Cezanne, beyond is Holbein and Rembrandt and Klimpt and Van Gogh. This gallery could challenge the Louvre or the British National Gallery. Look over there. . .Manet and Raphael and. . ." Marc suddenly stopped and turned his flushed face once more toward Ian.

"Do you know what this reminds me of?" Marc said in a low voice. Ian returned his gaze, as stunned as Marc was.

"I was thinking the same thing. This is a horde of art just like the Nazi stolen artworks in World War II," Ian frowned. "Lambert is a neo-Nazi, he's German, and he's turning the tables on the rest of the world. He's stealing back what the Third Reich was forced to return to all the museums they looted. It's restitution in reverse."

Marc snickered. "Yeah, and he's one crazy son of a bitch, too. Only a demented mind would dream up a stunt like this, much less actually try to carry it out."

"You have grossly underestimated me as usual, gentlemen," a loud voice boomed across the room, coming from a loud speaker somewhere near the roof. "You'll never catch me. I've been three steps ahead of you all the time, just as I am this very minute. We could have killed all of you on the way over here. Too bad your pitiful lives have to come to an end this way, locked away inside this apparently vacant building. I enjoyed our little game of hopscotch as long as it lasted. But I outsmarted you blue bloods, the famed Scotland Yard and the best of the American finest."

In a low voice, Marc urged Ian. "Go stand in front of the paintings, he won't shoot at us for fear of damaging the paintings. Move! Hurry before they cut loose with a fusillade of gunfire.""

Several trap doors opened in the high vaulted ceiling revealing guns pointed at the intruders. Shots began to spray across the room. One of the shots immediately killed Lambert's henchman, another one hit Ian in the thigh while another grazed Marc's head. The military guards were searching for the source of the shooting, but before they could return fire they too were gunned down one by one. Marc and Ian stood alone now at the mercy of a madman determined to kill all of them. Marc's first thoughts were of Erika and how devastated she would be to learn of his death.

"Too bad, Lieutenant," the voice boomed across the spacious room again, "you should have just given us the Mount Ranier painting and gone your way and you wouldn't have all these problems. Now it's you and me and you have no place to go. You should've known you can't get the best of me. Now no one will even know how you died. Maybe I'll add your dead body to my wax museum."

The staccato of machinegun fire split the air and another spray of bullets flew across the room hitting Ian in the chest and neck and striking Marc high in the chest and his left shoulder. Marc knew in an instant that Ian was dead, and if he wasn't careful he would be next if he didn't take care of his own wounds. In addition to the taste of blood in his mouth, he felt weakness starting to take over his body.

The floor was slippery now with blood oozing from his wounds, but he no longer could stand upright. Using the space between two paintings for a guide, he put his back to the wall and slid down to the floor attempting to sit upright, but by now he was losing focus and dizziness was beginning to surround him.

"It has taken years for me to build up this collection, "Lambert boasted, "and I'm still not finished. But that's only part of my master plan. I have hundreds and hundreds of specialists working for me to resurrect the Third Reich that I will rename *the Fourth Reich.*

You ignorant British and Americans destroyed my mother until she killed herself, and you murdered my father at Nuremberg by hanging him. Now I'm going to kill you, one by one. When I finally create the Fourth Reich, I will control all of Germany, then all of Europe. I will do it not with storm troops, but with lawyers and financiers and scientists already at work for me now underground. We have an endless supply of young women we can experiment with to create humans with abilities far beyond anything that exists today.

As we speak, some of the best surgeons are at work on these women to change female physical abilities to give birth to humans with extreme intelligence and physical proportions far beyond what was once considered normal. We created several females whose bodies are so beautiful that men cannot resist them. Our progress over the past years has been incredible. Already we've given birth to twenty-second century scientists and economic geniuses whose ideas and theories make Albert Einstein appear to be a low-grade idiot.

I will establish a new art world, a second renaissance devoted to beautiful paintings and sculpture, and Germany will become the most powerful nation in the world again. I will create completely new ideas in science and technology, and redesign today's concepts of the human mind and body that will astonish the miserable attempts of the world of today. That will be my masterpiece, and all of you are powerless to stop me. I will be the master of the world of tomorrow. Prepare to die now, I salute your puny plans to stop me."

Giving up the attempt to stay seated, Marc rolled over and laid his head on the carpeted floor. Sleep tried to steal wakefulness from him, yet he welcomed its soft touch to his body. Already the pistol had fallen from his hand and bounced against the blood-soaked carpet. Strangely, he wondered, why he didn't hear it fall from his hand. The room turned grey above him. Life had no more color to it. His eyelids were much too heavy to stay open.

The shouting of the madman Lambert reverberated off the walls and ceiling, ramblings and ravings about a new Fourth Reich uttered by a psychotic lunatic who was beyond all the confines of normalcy and human decency.

He thought he heard faint voices shouting and people moving around him, but nothing was part of him any longer. He gave in to a thick gray blanket of life and eagerly reached unavoidably for the darker black that now shut out all sound and sight. Death offered him a sickening smile, a beckoning hand to take from him all that he had left.

"You fools. . .you damn fools," Lambert laughed, "I own these works of art, and I WILL own them for the rest of my life! *Deutschland uber alles!*" Lambert shouted.

Marc was beyond hearing, beyond seeing. Only darkness now was recognizeable. He was growing colder, even the pain was taken away by a strengthening numbness. *What would Erika do now that he was gone*, Marc choked. He tried to cry, but the tears were held back by the hand of Death. The world turned black, completely void of everything, and at last he found the peaceful quiet he was yearning for.

Erika busied herself with her duties until suddenly she found Barker standing at her side. "We have a very serious problem on our hands," he approached her.

"I've been talking to one of the prisoners – he intimated the attack squad is walking into an ambush. Lambert and some snipers are waiting at the warehouse to kill them all. We have to act quickly, Erika, and even now it may be too late. It wasn't a good idea to send Ian and Marc together on the same raid. Lambert could kill them both at the same time."

"They'll be cut to pieces," she put her hands to her face. "Where's the Colonel, we have to go after them."

"We can reach them on the radio, let's go," Barker urged.

"No, no, they're under a radio silence blackout," she began to cry, "their radios aren't even turned on. Get the Colonel!" She ran from the room looking for Colonel Richards, finally catching up to him. "Colonel, Colonel," she shook his arm, "Barker says the attack squad is walking into a trap. What can we do, we have to warn them."

Taking a few moments to sort out the confusion, the Colonel outlined a plan that might get the rescue team to them before it was too late. The prisoner laughed out loud at their predicament.

"You fools," he taunted them, "Dufrey is trained to lead them into a trap. You can't outwit Lambert, I tell you, he's going to gun them down right where they stand."

"The plane they arrived in has a homing device," the Colonel reminded, "we should be picking them up anytime now. It's much like a GPS, but it can pinpoint their position exactly. I'll get a rescue team ready, we can use two helicopters, but we have to leave NOW," he emphasized.

With another squad of eight Rangers, they took off immediately, relying on the homing device as a beacon. They were at least forty-five minutes behind the first attack squad, but the helicopters should be able to cut down the time to about twenty minutes, so the Colonel thought. He reached over and squeezed Erika's arm. "Now, now, don't worry, we'll get there pretty fast; it's going to be alright."

Erika was beside herself with fear. "What if they don't get there soon enough and Marc and the first squad are killed outright. But maybe he'll only be wounded. He's tough, and he has Ian with him. Between the two of them, they'll find a way to survive." She dried her face with a handkerchief but just as quickly she began crying again.

"We've got 'em on the homing device, Colonel," the pilot shouted, "we have about fifteen minutes to go to catch up to them."

The Colonel shifted over to a seat beside their prisoner. "Okay, you miserable bastard, you better start talking or I'll kick you out the door at five thousand feet and watch you splatter all over somebody's roof top. Now what's it going to be?"

The prisoner stared horrified at the Colonel. "You wouldn't do that, it's not legal." Richards leaned over and jerked open the helicopter door just a little. The incoming blast of cool air hit both of them, shocking them to attention.

"Just try me, buddy, and you'll find out. We're playing by your rules now, and anything goes. Can you flap your arms and fly?" The Colonel gave the prisoner a slight bump as if to push him out the door.

"All right, all right," the prisoner squealed, "what do you want to know?"

"How far is the warehouse from the airfield?" Richards prodded him. "How long will it take us to go that distance in a bus?"

"About twenty minutes. It's a very difficult road that twists its way up the mountain side."

"Can you recognize the warehouse from the air? Can you get us right on top of it?"

"Yes, yes I can, it has a red roof and it's on the corner of three streets."

Richard dragged the prisoner up to the helicopter cockpit. "Lieutenant, this turkey says he can put us right on top of the warehouse."

"There's the plane," the pilot pointed out the window, "which way do we go from here?"

"Turn to the right now, go this way, it's not very far, about five minutes or so by air," the pilot calculated. In minutes, the helicopter landed in the street beside the warehouse. The squad's leader slipped cautiously inside the unguarded opening. Looking around the amazing room, the squad leader returned.

"The first squad is all dead; we'll have to fight our way into the building," the squad leader told them. "Go ahead, bust out the windows and the doors. Get in there as fast as you can," the Colonel urged them.

The squad of rangers and medics broke into the building in a rush, then stopped in their tracks. The Colonel, Erika and the prisoner followed close behind. The spectacle that greeted them was beyond shocking – bodies littered the floor, blood was everywhere. Worse than that, no one seemed to be alive. Erika screamed and rushed over to where Ian and Marc had fallen.

"Marc, Marc, oh dear God, no, no, not this, not Marc, too," she wailed and dropped to the floor beside him. "Marc, Marc, can you hear me?" she called out to him between sobs. She reached for him and shook his body, then leaned over and covered him with her own body. The medics had to pry her away from him.

"Please, ma'am, we need to look at him, please," they begged. She finally relented and gave him up to the medics, but in her heart she thought he was already dead.

Another team of medics bent over Ian momentarily, until they realized he was already dead. Then they inspected all the other bodies. Erika merely sat on the floor, unable to stand on her feet. The tears and sobs had quieted and her face became a stone mask. Without moving, she stared straight ahead of her, not seeing what was in front of her. She fell over sideways and lost consciousness.

"Colonel, this one's still alive, only just barely," a medic turned to Richards. "We need to get him to a hospital fast."

The medics worked over Marc for nearly half and hour until he was ready to be transported. Quickly they put Marc and Ian on stretchers and headed for the helicopter, strapping Erika to the seats and holding her in place while they tried to revive her. Colonel Richards stared out the window at the lights passing below, wishing the day had never happened and sensing that this was one of the worst days of his life.

After a week in the hospital and four major surgeries, Marc still lay in a coma. The hospital staff moved a second bed into his room for Erika, who refused to leave his side. During all that time she remained silent, draped across his body with her hands holding his. She ate little food between fits of sobbing, sleeping occasionally in little pieces of time.

The hospital staff once in a while tried to encourage her to slow down her vigil, but with little success. They gave her vitamin shots now and then to keep her strength up, but for the most part she simply remained motionless. Her life was coming to an end. If Marc died in spite of all the attempts to save him, she would have nothing to live for, and the promises of life would simply vanish.

Well into the second week, nurses changed bandages again, attached new drip bottles, sometimes trying to replace various bed sheets and otherwise went about their usual chores. It was during one of these sessions that Marc moved his hand ever so slightly. Erika felt the movement and jumped to her feet, calling the nurses' attention to his hand.

"He moved his hand, I felt it move!" she cried. "Does that mean he's waking up?"

"It could have been involuntary, but you need to watch him closely," a nurse said and left the room. Erika lay closer to him now, hoping and praying he was beginning to shrug off the coma. An hour later, she felt his hand move again. She grabbed the call button and kept pressing it until the nurse appeared in the room.

"Did he move again?" she asked. "Yes, yes, I felt it move ever so slowly. Shouldn't we call a doctor?" The nurse whisked herself out of the room without answering, returning a moment later with the attending physician who took Marc's hand and waited. Marc moved his hand again slightly, and then his knee. Erika saw the sheet move across his knee and she burst into tears. "He's waking, I know he is, he's going to be all right!"

For the next two hours, the doctor kept watch trying not to get Erika's hopes up. Another doctor came into the room and recorded Marc's vital signs.

"His vitals are getting stronger, I think he's about to wake up," the doctor speculated. Marc's eyelids fluttered and he mumbled something indistinguishable. Several moments later he spoke Erika's name, softly at first and then in an almost normal tone of voice.

"I'm here, Marc, I'm here right beside you, darling. Don't try to talk, just look at me and I'll know what you're trying to say. Don't get in a hurry, love, take it slow and easy. Oh my darling, you're going to be all right, you'll be all right. Tears ran down her cheeks in little ribbons of human water as she buried her face in the bed sheets. All she cared about at this moment was that he was alive. Then he tried to say her name. "Erka. . . Erka," he mumbled over and over.

For Erika, life suddenly was worth living again and her tears became great sobs of joy. A tiny motion of his lips told her he was trying to smile. No brilliant sunshine could ever be as bright as that first tiny smile. Several weeks passed while he grew stronger and began to speak in whole sentences, then started holding conversations and eating meals. She told him about the attack on the warehouse and Ian's death, relating the story of the rescue and the dash to the hospital.

He listened mostly in silence, occasionally staring out the window. The day finally arrived when Erika could walk him down the corridor, then around the entire floor, and at last beside him as he walked by himself. "Look at this!" he guffawed, "no more cane, I can walk on my own thanks to you, sweetheart."

While Marc convalesced, he still offered his ideas about the Lambert organization. Scotland Yard, the FBI and other law enforcement agencies continued to put more and more pieces of the puzzle together. Occasional meetings were held in his hospital room. The "puzzle" as it was now called was nearly closed and the law enforcement agencies were brought up to date. Marc was released from the hospital and life began to return to normal.

After a few weeks more, Marc and Erika dropped by the Scotland Yard offices to meet the new Chief Inspector under better circumstances. "I'm so glad to finally meet you," Erika smiled, "we've heard good things about you."

"Well, you've become quite a legend around here," Bill Simmons shook Marc's hand. "It's bad enough I have to fill Ian's shoes, but I could never fill your shoes. And this is the little lady who started all this, I'm so happy to see you, too. This is providential, two celebrities at one time. I must be doing something right."

"Don't believe everything you hear," Marc said, "somebody's public relations is working overtime. I'm just a guy trying to do a job, which reminds me, what do we hear from that Nazi idiot Lambert?"

"Well he hasn't stopped yet, if that's what you're referring to," Simmons reflected. "While you were convalescing, his gang struck again – at St. Giles Cathedral in Edinburgh, and once more at the Rijksmuseum in Amsterdam. Luckily no one was killed, but a few chaps got banged up a bit."

Simmons continued to tap his pencil against the top of the table. "These are the world's most prestigious museums and buildings, including some of the most sophisticated security systems. How does he consistently manage to break through those security systems?"

Marc lounged back in his chair. "If you have a few minutes, I'd like to talk about that gang. I have some ideas I'd like to explore."

"I'd like to hear those ideas, Marc. Frankly, I'm quite puzzled by the whole affair in spite of the background I've been able to gather."

The three of them settled back. Simmons ordered up some tea, and they got down to serious business.

St. Giles Cathedral Interior, Edinburgh, Scotland

"First a couple of questions, if you don't mind," Marc began. "Did the gang move all the artwork?"

"Yes, and mighty fast, too," Simmons frowned. "Our team went back three days later to take inventory and the warehouse was totally empty. I can't imagine how he was able to accomplish that. Where's Sherlock Holmes when we need him?"

"I suspected as much," Marc waved his hand. "And the second question — has there even been a hint about where Lambert's stronghold is, or whatever his real name is?"

"Sadly, not a word on both counts," Simmons apologized. "It's almost as though he just vanished except for the two raids I mentioned. I can see the wheels in your head are turning again, Marc, what are you thinking?"

"I vowed to get him," Marc said passionately, "and I fully intend to keep that promise. I have personal reasons which I won't go into, but he might as well recognize the truth — the bastard's days are numbered." Erika sat straight up with a sudden short gasp.

"Marc, you can't do that, you're not ready, I can't believe you'd even consider it. We almost lost you once, now you want to go off on a tangent and open yourself up to who knows what. Please, honey, don't get hurt again."

"Surely you can't be serious," Simmons sat forward, "not in your present condition, old boy. You might not make it next time, you know, you're still much too weak to get involved."

"Maybe so," Marc spoke up, "but there's nothing wrong with my head — I can still think, and my instincts tell me he's putting forward his greatest boast now, which weakens his ability to succeed. We're going to let his pride do him in. Nothing ruins a man more than his ego. We're going to hit him hardest of all this time and we're going to do it right out in public. He won't be able to resist — he'll literally be driven to defend himself, to keep his name clear. But right now, we need some really good intel. That's where you come in, Bill."

Simmons leaned forward frowning. "What do you have in mind, Marc?"

"First: let's set up the War Room again as our Command Post with Class A+ security," Marc began. "No one in or out without tight security check."

"Second: anyone working on this operation MUST be working on a *need to know* basis.

"Third: every full time employee who works in the War Room MUST have ocular – eye ball - clearance and fingerprint admittance, and cannot carry a physical entrance card.

"Fourth: two armed guards will be posted at the door of the War Room night and day.

"Fifth: all electronic wires leading to and from the War Room will be thoroughly checked randomly twice a day, without the knowledge of the War Room workforce.

"Sixth: we're going to hold a press conference and point the finger at Lambert – and make fun of him, laugh at him, tell the public how stupid he is, and then wait for him to respond.

In the meantime, pick your four best undercover agents and turn them loose on Lambert. We need to find his stronghold, raid it, and flush him out into the open where we can arrest him. We also need to locate his new warehouse with all the paintings, and this time seal it off from Lambert so he can't reclaim the stolen artwork."

"I say, Marc," Simmons asked hesitantly, "don't you think this is a bit excessive? I mean, even members of Parliament wouldn't be able to get admittance."

"Exactly, that's the point, Bill. On three occasions, Lambert's men have broken through our security. If we are to survive, it can't be allowed to happen again. We're faced now with a life or death situation if we're to stop Lambert. This must be all or nothing."

A sudden knock on the door brought Colonel Richards into the discussion.

"I have a piece of news that's going to make you dance in the streets," he smiled with a twinkle in his eye. "We've bugged the holding cells for two of Lambert's men we captured a while back. I think I know where his stronghold might be, and you're not going to believe it." Everyone sat up straight in expectation, almost breathless in anticipation.

"Scotland Yard has been doing quite a bit of investigating," Richards began, "following Lambert's henchmen as well as Lambert himself." The Colonel looked over at Simmons. "Your boys deserve a pat on the back, Bill, they did a masterful job this time. Are you ready?" Everyone nodded in assent.

"It's in Lucerne. We've put all the little pieces together and confirmed and confirmed again our findings. Then we sent out several patrols of mountain climbers until we had success. There's a mountain in Lucerne accessible by a cog railway and a cable car for the tourists. It's Mount Pilatus, a seven-thousand-foot mountain with a resort hotel at the top, named in honor of Pontius Pilate.

Then we sent out undercover troops who caught a glimpse of the man we're looking for. Lambert owns half that resort for his hideaway. We've followed him inside several times and we know how he gets inside and out without being seen. Of course, he wears a multitude of disguises, but we still can tag him and see where he goes."

"Colonel, you're a genius," Marc's eyes narrowed. "If this is true, we've got the bastard dead to rights."

"Oh it's true, alright," Richards continued. "And we also know where his warehouse is – it's right there in Lucerne as well."

"I think we could pull off a coordinated attack if we plan it right," Marc's brain was racing now, "but we'd need to plan it right down to the second if we're going to get our rabbit in the trap. Why don't we call it *Code Name Pilatus*?" They all agreed in a mix of eager voices.

"This plan will have to be more secret than the *Manhattan Project* – the atomic bomb – and as coordinated as the attack of a rattlesnake bite. But it can be done," Marc offered.

"Well, let's get started," Simmons suggested, "it's going to take some time to put all this together into a workable plan, so we'd better get moving."

"Think we can be ready in two weeks?" Erika questioned. "This is going to take a lot of manpower, it's pretty complex, and I'm not sure Marc is completely up to it yet."

Marc turned toward Erika. "I can do it with your help. We'll need Bill to break through some obstacles early on. Why don't you and I start with the War Room? And let's get Simmons going on a public news conference that belittles Lambert."

Within a short time, Scotland Yard Chief Inspector Simmons stood at a podium outside the Yard headquarters in front of a dozen microphones and as many television cameras. He paused a moment or two, thinking to himself *this better be convincing.* He took a deep breath. Reading from his prepared script, he launched into his statement.

"I wish to make a short statement at this time about the numerous thefts of artworks and weapons that have plagued no less than eight nations in the past twelve months.

Scotland Yard now confirms that special investigators have been tracking the arch criminal Gustav Blaatner, leader of an international gang of European thieves and murderers. We are pleased to announce that this leader, because of his inability and recklessness, is now cornered in Switzerland and is awaiting arrest for his crimes against a number of European countries over the past year.

Blaatner, alias Mr. Lambert, lost control of his gang members and began making so many mistakes in his activities that his trail became quite easy to follow. Together with highly experienced officers of Scotland Yard, we are able to compile a lengthy list of robberies and murders and are moments away from putting this stupid man Blaatner into handcuffs. Blaatner's pitiful planning and the foolish execution of his activities allows Scotland Yard to make a long list of charges that guarantee a life behind bars for the rest of his life."

"I have a suggestion before we get started," Simmons leaned over toward Marc, "Have you ever been hypnotized, like we did with Erika?" "Yes, but it was a long time ago," Marc answered. "What are you thinking?"

Simmons leaned closer. "Do you remember anything Lambert was saying before you were shot? I mean, anything recognizable you could repeat?"

"Just bits and pieces," Marc responded, "a word or two here and there. I was intent on surviving the sharpshooters in the warehouse. I guess I was in shock when I realized Ian Brooks was dead and I was dying after being hit three times. You think I might remember more under hypnosis?"

"Let me get Doctor Wentworth back and see if he can get you to pull out those words. There might be something we can use."

The doctor sat in front of Marc and began his procedure. In a few moments, Marc was in a deep trance and, at the doctor's direction, began to relive the moments he laid on the floor wounded. The doctor's voice became softer and softer, then coaxing Marc to remember.

"You're asleep now; you're feeling the quiet peace of today, reaching for Lambert's voice to hear what he is saying. Do you remember Lambert's voice now? What's he saying – what words do you recognize?"

Marc stirred in his chair. ". . . mother killed herself. . .murdered father Nuremberg Trials. . . Fourth Reich. . . Germany . . .lawyers. . .scientists. . .second renaissance. . .new science . . .new technologies. . .creating new mind and body. . .masterpiece. . .rule the world. . .kill us all. . ."

Marc twisted in his chair and became agitated. His voice slowly grew louder and shaky and he wrung his hands as perspiration broke out on his face.

"Marc, can you hear my voice?" the doctor asked.

"Yes, your voice, far off."

"I can't let him relive that whole scenario," the doctor cautioned everyone, "he's getting agitated. I'm going to count backwards from five to one, Marc," the doctor said. "When I reach one, you will wake up, okay?"

"Yes," Marc replied.

"Five – four – three – two – one."

Marc blinked his eyes several times and turned his head. "Did I tell you something, did it work?"

"You were magnificent, Marc," Dr.Wentworth was jubilant, "you just gave us all the missing pieces we've been looking for so long. Now we know who Blaatner really is. His background has jumped up and bit him where it hurts. So he's planning a new world order with himself as the number one. He's a neo-Nazi and all his activities have been aimed at that one goal. Now it's time to spring into action."

"Marc, we've solved the whole puzzle," Simmons beamed, "all the answers. Why didn't we try this method a long time ago? Are you okay now, partner?"

Marc slumped down in his chair. "I'm a little tired, I just need to rest a moment."

"Take your time, don't get in a rush," Simmons repeated.

"You won't believe what you said, honey," Erika was overjoyed.

"I. . .I sort of remember some things now," Marc coughed, "about his anger and his parents. That's what caused him to develop his psychopathology; his father was judged guilty at the Nuremberg Trials when he was a very small boy. He keeps reliving that entire trauma over and over again, especially the fact that his mother hanged herself. Now he wants revenge, no matter what the cost and no matter who gets caught in the crossfire."

British Fast Train, England

veryone worked day and night at their separate plans until, little by little, the once elusive pieces all fell into place as a master plan. Simmons called a preliminary meeting of the five of them after three weeks work – Chief Inspector Simmons, Marc, Erika, Colonel Richards, and Deputy Chief Inspector Barker. Close to exhaustion, they all flopped down in chairs around the conference table in the War Room.

"Let's get started so we can get to bed early," Simmons said, "we can start with Erika and Marc."

"The War Room is completely ready," Marc started. "Security is so tight an ant couldn't get in without an eyeball and fingerprint check. Two armed guards at the door on the outside rotating four hour shifts, then two more inside the door with the same time rotation. We'll be receiving communications from all over Europe and North America. The inside of the War Room was designed by Erika, so she can take it from here."

"Once again, entrance is only by eyeball and fingerprint," Erika indicated. "All work posts are on eight hour shifts. I need one more week to install soundproof walls round about, and to train the workers I've already chosen. I'll set up classes and teach everyone myself.

All wiring leading into and out of the building are underground and encased in protective tubing. There are ten computer positions, each protected by three separate virus-killers and also a 'check-any-time' hacker finder. Telephone systems are fixed with a 'go-to' pick-up to Interpol. A single large screen monitor can project two-way views of the people talking to each other.

Each work position has a dumb bell button that automatically shuts down all the computers simultaneously if one of the workers detects an outside invader. Latrines are installed inside the War Room — once a worker enters the War Room, she or he has no reason to leave until their shift is over. Meals are furnished by caterers four times a day. All I need now is the date for the attack and I'll be ready whenever that time comes. Colonel Richards, it's your turn."

"Okay, heads up, this might seem a little complicated at first," the Colonel spoke up. "Troops from the 82nd Airborne Division have joined with the British 6th Airborne Division to form one unit commanded by British Colonel Walter Anderson. Both divisions currently are in training for airdrops on the Pilatus Kulm, the hotels, on top of the mountain. Depending on the weather, the troops will airdrop from either helicopter or low-flying aircraft.

Part of the combined division also will drop on and take over simultaneously both the gondola and the cog railway, and secure both locations. Troops from both American and British divisions are trained for mountain climbing as well as combat — sixty troops at each of the three locations — Pilatus Kulm, cog railway, and gondola. Two days from the appointed time, all civilians will be evacuated from the three locations under the pretense of emergency maintenance work.

All troops are ordered to engage the enemy with extreme force, except Mr. Lambert who is to be captured alive at all cost. If he is in disguise, it will be a difficult call, but the troops will do the best they can. They have been shown some of the disguises he's used in the past. Capturing prisoners is also stressed with the troops. If you can stop them by disabling them and taking them prisoner, so much the better than just killing them outright.

So, we're ready for the signal whenever it comes. By the way, all troops have been advised that this mission is designated a *no fail* mission. Oh . . .I almost forgot. We have a printed leaflet ready to be posted at all the hotels at ground level as well as the Pilatus Kulm resort on top the mountain, and at the Cog Railway and Gondola take-off points. The postings can go up within three hours when the date and time are agreed, and are printed up by the British 6th Airborne Division.

"I say, well done, Colonel," Simmons said with a smile. "Marc and Jim Barker, your turn now."

"Our role in this is the creation of lockdown security and overall intelligence gathering," Marc began. "Anyone – ANYONE – associated with this enterprise has been advised that it is a maximum security effort, which means any small part comes with the assurance that security is a number-one predetermined policy. Lambert has his own definition of security, so you can be sure he has his own plan already in effect. Also, if you need intel relating to a single matter, you can ask either of us to help you out.

We have a decent view of Lambert's employee count – at least the employees he uses on a daily basis, including his guards. That number is about forty-five. Remember that he out-sources a widespread number of one-time employees for specific single jobs."

"Marc and I are a clearing house for intelligence," Barker added. "At the moment, we're in touch with MI6, Interpol and intel groups in Scotland, Amsterdam, Lucerne, Berlin, Munich, Cologne, Belgium, and Vienna. That is to say, we coordinate efforts among these groups.

Right now, Lambert's laying low – we think he suspects something is brewing on our part. If we keep security tight, he won't learn anything about us. In the meantime, we just need to keep building our strength and keep sharpening the sword. We have a good understanding of Lambert's organization and what to expect in terms of overt activity. I'm sure he is presently in a defensive posture, trying to determine where we will strike first."

"It seems we're about at readiness," Simmons calculated. "All we need do now is set the date and time for attack. I'm waiting for a weather forecast that should be coming through momentarily. We don't want to get everything scrambled by an early snow."

The telephone rang and Simmons picked it up. After a few moments, he put the phone back in its cradle and looked around the room.

"Good news, the weather chaps say we're okay for about a week or ten days. Anyone have any last minute concerns? As for the public news conference, I'll handle it on newspapers, radio and television. Lambert will be furious at the way we have portrayed him as a dunce. That will force him into making mistakes, such as forgetting about the small details of his own plan."

Simmons looked about the room once more. "Let's take a poll then. When I call out your function, just answer *Go or No Go*.

One by one, each leader waited for his call: Airborne Troops – Aircraft - War Room – Intelligence – Communications – Cog Railway – Gondola – Intel - Covert Ops.

"Let's make one check just for test," Simmons advised. "Where is Lambert at this very moment?" Everyone reached for a telephone, then answered in turn. In summary, their answers were all the same – in his stronghold atop Pilatus.

"Good, now for the date and time," Simmons cautioned again. "Don't forget, civilians have to be evacuated so they'll need two days notice. I say August 28 at 1400 hours, that's a week from now," Simmons suggested. Everyone agreed.

Simmons pointed to their telephones. "Alright, ladies and gentlemen, send out the word and we're on our way. There's no turning back. *Code Name Pilatus* is set for August 28 at 2:00pm in the afternoon. In the words of Tiny Tim, may God bless us everyone."

Civilian evacuation is set for August 24 announcement, actual begins the following day. I suggest each of you in this room take two days time off to rest up, you're going to need all the strength you have when H-Hour begins. Let your staffs hang on 'til you get back."

After the meeting, Marc pulled Colonel Richards aside. "Colonel, I have a large but unofficial favor to ask of you."

"Of course, Marc, what do you need?" Marc took a deep breath.

"Is it possible for Erika and me to comandeer a helicopter and a pilot for a two day trip to Wales? I know this is asking a great deal, Ted, but we need to take two days in Wales before the fireworks starts."

The Colonel rubbed his chin a moment, then looked over at Marc. "It can be done, but I'll need to negotiate it with you. I'll authorize it, but only if you promise on a stack of bibles that you'll marry this girl when our *little picnic* is over. Can you do that?"

Marc was overjoyed. "Well, I intend to do that anyway. I've already waited too long to ask her, but it depends on whether she'll have me. Tell you what, Colonel, if she turns me down, I'll pay for the gasoline."

"It's a deal," Richards chuckled, "but I still think you're getting the better part of this deal. I've seen the way she looks at you and, confidentially, I wish I'd met a woman who looked at me the way she looks at you. When do you want to start?"

"Immediately - if not sooner," Marc shot back.

"Okay, get out to the airfield as quick as you can. Ask for Major Parker, he'll be authorized to go wherever you tell him. And for pete's sake, pop the question while you're on holiday — just wish I could be there when you do."

Mark slapped the Colonel on the back, grabbed Erika by the hand, and rushed out the door.

★ ★ ★

Their helicopter landed on the beach at Tenby, the pilot agreeing to be back at the appointed time.

"I already have an overnight room reserved for us along with a reservation at our favorite seaside café. Let's get moving."

"You think of everything, don't you?" Erika giggled.

At the hotel, they took a shower together and stretched out in bed. "I'm worried about you with this attack coming up," Erika said. "You always take too many chances, sweetheart, promise me you won't do that until Lambert's in the slammer."

"I'll be careful, don't worry. Right now all I want to do is forget the battle and hold you in my arms. It seems such a long time since we've been able to curl up together."

"Much too long," she whispered. "Now stop talking and kiss me again."

She overwhelmed him in bed, caressing his whole body. "Erika, I love you so very much, and I miss you when I'm away from you for only a few minutes. No woman I ever met fills my heart with such feelings. I guess you know you're stuck with me for life."

"I hope so, and I hope you'll always love me the way I love you now."

She put her fingers on his lips. "Shhhh, you're talking too much again. And I want you to know that I never want to be alone without you, never! Now we're both talking too much. Shhhh." With that, they came together and sealed their love once again with promises of *forever* as the afternoon wore on.

As the day turned to evening, they took a long walk on the beach and sat side-by-side at their favorite café. "Happy, darling?" he asked. "Unbelievably so," she cooed.

"There's something I need to talk to you about," Marc said gently.

"What's that?" she asked. He turned full toward her and took her hand in his.

"I've noticed you can get a little wild now and then," he said laughing, "but are you crazy enough to marry me? Will you marry me, Erika, so we can be together forever and forever?"

Her arms shot around his neck and they held each other tightly. "What's taking you so long to answer?" he questioned.

"I don't want you to think I'm a pushover," she smiled at him with a single tear sliding down her cheek, then relented. "Of course I'll marry you, tough guy, what took you so long to ask me? I can't hold my breath any longer."

"Oh, wow!" he said out loud, "I was scared to death you'd say 'no'," he choked out the words. "Think you won't mind being married to a cop?"

Beaches at Tenby, Wales

"You're making a cop out of me!" she blurted out. "I'll never be satisfied pounding a computer keyboard anymore. Coming over here forced me to learn new skills and take new risks. Trying to keep up with you isn't easy."

"Well," Marc thought a moment, "we don't have to go back to St. Louis, you know. Maybe we'll find a completely new life over here. There's a huge world out there just for the taking. Think about it."

"I've been thinking about something else," she spoke up. "We're ready now to spring our attack, and it's going to be a little rough. Is there a reason you decided to propose to me at this particular time? Are you worried one of us may get badly hurt, or even killed? What if both of us don't survive, or maybe only one of us survives and the other one gets killed. Did that have anything to do with your decision right now to ask me?"

Marc looked down into her eyes and thought about what he was going to say.

"No, honey, that never entered my mind. I proposed just now because it's what I wanted to do, not because I'm afraid one or both of us won't make it through alive. I proposed because I love you and I want you to be my wife."

Erika let her breath out slowly. "I just wondered about that all of a sudden."

"Now that you mention it," Marc added, "it's possible for one of us to get mortally wounded – maybe both of us – but I keep thinking about our future together. When this is all over, we'll have some decisions to make about where we want to live and what we want to do with the rest of our lives. I don't really think about the worst that could happen, I think about the attack working so well we won't ever have to worry about it again."

"I'm so glad you have that kind of approach on your mind - so do I," Erika smiled.

"The guy at bat doesn't think about striking out," Marc continued. "He thinks about hitting a home run. If he was worried about striking out, then he shouldn't be playing the game."

She wrapped her arms around his neck. "I feel the same way," she came back, "so let's just think about doing our jobs. Anyway, we still have another day to enjoy ourselves."

10

Back at the War Room, Marc and Erika set themselves to work preparing for the signal to unleash the attack. Erika polled the principal leaders once more, confirming each one's readiness status. Marc contacted each intelligence agency in turn, polling their readiness status, at last satisfied that all was well. He looked up to find Simmons standing at his elbow.

"All is in readiness, Bill," he greeted Simmons with his usual smile, rubbing his hands together. Looking into Simmons' face, Marc could see the man was troubled about something. "Easy does it, Bill, don't look so worried, everyone is prepared."

"My secretary didn't come to work yesterday," the words came tumbling out of Simmons' mouth, "and she never called in sick. That's very strange because she isn't like that, she's very organized. I called her home at the end of the day, but there was no answer. She's not here today, either, and there was no answer when I called her house. What do you think about that?"

"I don't know, Bill, you know her better than anyone," Marc commented. "Send someone to her house if you think something's amiss."

"I did, I'm waiting for him to call back now."

"Mr. Simmons, this package just arrived for you, delivered by hand," an officer said, handing over the package. Simmons ripped open the package and retrieved a note written by hand. Simmons frowned and handed the note to Marc.

'We all lead lives of quiet desperation' the philosopher wrote.

"What does that mean?" Simmons looked up. He peeked down into the package and retrieved a lock of brown hair from the envelope. The lock of hair had been dipped in blood.

"Good Lord," Simmons exclaimed.

"What color is Miss Worthington's hair, Bill?" Marc quietly asked.

"Brown, just like this lock of hair," Simmons responded, grabbing up his radiophone and calling. After a few minutes, he put the phone down and shouted. "Carl, get over to Miss Worthington's house, see what's going on, hurry! I sent Terry over there to find Miss Worthington, but he doesn't answer his radio."

"I'll be back shortly," Simmons told Marc and disappeared out the door of the War Room. He returned stone-faced in fifteen minutes.

"The house was unlocked, and Terry's body was lying on the living room floor, dead. He'd been shot several times. Scrawled on the wall in blood were the letters *ETC – ETC– ETC.*"

The calm posture of the War Room was shattered by Erika's scream. "Marc – Bill, come over and look at this, hurry."

The two men stared at the photograph in her hand with disbelief. It showed Miss Worthington naked, tied to a chair and gagged so she couldn't scream. Her body was smeared with blood in several places and the region below her stomach was bathed in a pool of blood but she was still alive. Scrawled on the wall in blood behind her was the single sentence, ***Give Up Or She Dies – You Have 24 Hours***.

Marc looked up at Simmons. The Yard inspector's face was nearly white, as if the blood had been drained from it. "Look at her," Simmons said almost in a whisper. "Has he been torturing her? He'll kill her for sure. What can we do?"

He looked back at Marc with a single tear sliding down his cheek.

"I've just asked her to marry me, Marc, and she said 'yes', but he'll kill her. We're two days from H-hour, there are more than five hundred agents and combat troops waiting to jump off on signal, and we're moments away from getting our hands on Lambert. How can we possibly save her in time?"

Marc thought for a few minutes. "We don't have many options; in fact, we don't have any options at all." He looked over at Simmons. "It's your call, Bill. We'll do whatever you want us to do."

Simmons fell into a chair with his head in his hands. "No matter what we do, she's done for." He thought for another few minutes. "Good Lord, what she must have endured!"

"Is everyone on standby?" Simmons suddenly asked. "If we attack immediately, can we get to her in time? But we don't even know where he's holding her, it could be at several different places." Simmons thought for several more minutes. "Can we attack in the next five minutes, Marc?"

Marc turned to Erika. "Take a quick poll, I'll do the same, we want to know if everyone can attack immediately. Do it quick."

They both went to the telephones and polled their different groups. After about ten minutes, they had their answers. Marc looked over at Simmons who still had his head buried in his hands.

"It's a go, Bill, don't you want to order it right now?"

"Yes. . .yes, for heaven's sake, now, go, go, go!" Erika and Marc both picked up their phones and sent out the order: *Code Name Pilatus* is a GO NOW!

Marc, Erika and Simmons rushed for the doorway and into a waiting helicopter bound for Lucerne. All over Lucerne and up to the top of Mt. Pilatus, combat troops and law enforcement agents closed in on their quarry.

Both ends of the Pilatus cog railway were quickly shut down by armed troops of the British 6th Airborne Division. Lambert's ground level offices were invaded by British troops that broke through the doorways and herded office employees outside and into waiting buses, guarded by paratroops. The entire building was then shut down, telephone and other electric lines were cut and double guards posted at all entrances.

At the top of the mountain, sixty troops from the American 82nd Airborne Division dropped down from helicopters, surrounding the Lambert stronghold. Gunfire erupted all across the top of Pilatus, reverberating off the steep sides of the entire mountain range. Marc and Simmons could hear voices shouting in the distance.

Marc adjusted his binoculars to pick out various firefights and landmarks, then passed the eyeglasses to Erika and Simmons. In forty minutes, the building was invaded and disabled. Each separate office was inspected – civilians rounded up and herded into a large auditorium – every possible closet, toilet facility, cloakroom, and cafeteria space was evacuated. As quiet settled over the Pilatus pinnacle, bright orange flares arced through the skies signaling the attack was completed.

Lucerne against Mount Pilatus background

Marc's radiophone crackled. "Command, this is Major Jackson, 82nd Airborne."

"Send your message, Major," Marc answered

"Mount Pilatus is secured," the Major said. "The entire complex is invaded, civilians are evacuated and contained. Twelve enemy defenders are killed. No civilian casualties and no 82nd casualties, but three wounded. We're going through the civilian population now, no sign of Lambert yet. Someone from Command Center oughta come up here, this is some kind of stronghold. British 6th Airborne is checking out the civilian group. It must have cost this guy millions to set this up. Will call back after another security sweep. Out."

"Copy that, Major," Marc replied, "good job. See you later at the rally point. Out."

Marc cursed. "Don't tell me that bastard got away," he spit the words out. "We also have undercover operatives up there mingling with the civilians. Surely somebody's gonna find him in the middle of all that mess."

"Patience, Marc, he'll turn up," Simmons reminded.

At both ends of the Cog Railway, short scuffles broke out and occasionally a shot split the silence, telling Simmons that military troops had to shoot someone who was trying to get away using a railway car. Aside from that, each end of the railway and the gondola cars were quiet. Long parades of buses formed a steady string of prisoners being taken down the mountainside on their way to a designated school gymnasium serving as a roundup pen. Occasionally, short reports came into Command Center giving various details of the many operations underway.

Cog Railway loading area, Alpnachstad, Lucerne

"Command Center, this is Leftenant Morgan at the Office Building, over."

Simmons took the call. "Go ahead, Leftenant, this is Command Center," he replied.

"We have a serious problem, sir," the officer began. "The employees refuse to leave the building. Some of them are sitting on the floor refusing to move. We can get them out the hard way, even if we have to carry them. Request permission to use carryout maneuver and handcuffs."

"Permission granted," Simmons replied, "but make sure you get them all out. Preserve all records and computers. Out."

"Mayday, Mayday," came a frantic call over the radiophones. "This is 6th Airborne Division, found evidence of booby traps, request ambulances and buses asap. Situation critical."

"This is Command Center," Simmons answered the frantic call. "Hospitals notified, buses on the way. Hang on, the booby traps could go off any moment. Get those people out of there."

In the next instant, there was a huge explosion. Billows of black smoke and orange secondary explosions filled the skies over the office complex at ground level. From their Command position, Erika, Marc and Simmons could hear the screams and cries of Lambert's employees, trapped in the burning building.

"Good Lord," Simmons cried, "this is going to be a catastrophe, I'd better get over there. I can already smell the C4 explosions all the way over here. Lambert must have double-packed the C4 explosives." Simmons started off at a run and disappeared out of sight. Marc and Erika held their positions and waited for further transmissions by radio.

"Command Center, this is 82nd Airborne, some defenders found in air passages and duct work on top of Pilatus. Shots fired."

"Copy that, 82nd," Erika answered. "Make a complete security sweep again. Check for secret passageways. Lambert not identified yet."

"Roger that, Command, will do."

View of Cog Railway, Mount Pilatus

Lucerne resembled a combat zone. Military personnel carriers, ambulances, groups of troops, the sky filled with billowing smoke, occasional shots being fired, civilians in handcuffs — all mixed together. The scene for miles around gave every indication that an armed conflict had overtaken the mountaintop in addition to the landscape at the foot of the mountain.

"C'mon, Erika," Marc took her by the arm, "we need to get to the top of Pilatus; the invasion was a success, but the aftermath is getting pretty dicey. Let's get a Cog Railway car."

The cars at the bottom were doubled up with three in a row. They took the closest one and arrived at the top of Pilatus after several minutes. They could smell the stinging fumes of guns having been fired. Windows of the hotel here and there were broken out. In other places, flattened doorways attested to the attack by the 82nd Airborne troops.

"Where's the prisoner group?" Marc asked a soldier who pointed to a cluster of men and women off to the side. Erika and Marc moved toward the group and began looking at each individual, one by one.

"He's not here," Marc's voice was a mixture of frustration and anger. "How could he have got away, Erika, we planned for every possible event?"

"Well, then he's still in the building and they just haven't found him yet. Let's go inside the hotel and poke around," Erika answered. They encountered the guard at the door, who showed them how to get to Lambert's portion of the building.

"We have both his secretaries in custody if you want to question them," the guard said. "No, not right now," Marc said, "maybe later. On second thought, maybe we should see them. Send them in here as soon as you find them.

Once inside, they were amazed at the furnishings. A dozen computers and two sixty-inch wall-mounted monitors ringed one portion of a very large room. It was Lambert's view of the world. The kitchen area was filled with gadgets and cabinets for every conceivable delight. Beyond that, the plush bedroom consisted of a few chairs and storage closets, and an enormous bed. Photographs and paintings on the walls were of naked men and women in every imaginable sexual position.

"This ought to give you an idea of how sick he is," Erika shook her head. "I'll bet he took all these pictures himself. Here's a photo of a naked woman on a surgical table with him standing over her. You can tell by her facial expression she isn't sedated. Do you think he really enjoyed torturing women?"

"At least," Marc replied. "His psychopath and sociopath tendencies have absolutely no boundaries."

Mount Pilatus Hotel and Resort

They were interrupted by three guards accompanying Lambert's secretaries. Erika looked over at the two women.

"Were you his close secretaries all the time?" Marc asked. "Yes," they both answered. "Would you say he was a normal man?" Marc continued. "If you want to use the word secretary," one of them answered. "We were everything for him, and he was far from normal. The things he made us do would put him in an institution in any normal world."

"What do you mean?"

"We weren't ever allowed to wear clothes, and we had to help him mutilate the women he captured," one of them answered. "He made one of us take pictures while he was conducting the mutilations."

"Tell me what all that means," Marc pressed on, "did he cut them up without using anesthetics?"

"Yes, it was horrible, the way they screamed, I still have nightmares, and when they screamed he beat them. He never wore clothes during the mutilations and . . . he made us touch him all over while he cut them up."

"Didn't you try to escape somehow?" Marc queried.

"No, part of the time he had us locked in our rooms, and he beat us if we tried to escape. Most of the time we had to wear ankle chains. H e came to us all hours of the day and night and demanded us to perform for him. He was insatiable."

"Okay, that's enough, we don't need to hear any more," Marc finished up and had the guards take them away. "I thought I'd heard it all," he added, "but this is the worst kind of anger and bestiality I've ever heard."

Erika found another doorway and slowly turned the handle. Inside, she switched the lights on and stood staring at the contents of the room. Not an especially large room, it was filled with airtight display cases. She went to the nearest case and looked at its contents. Suddenly she screamed and put her hand to her mouth. Marc heard the scream and came running, encircling her in his arms.

"Erika. . .Erika. . .what's wrong," he pleaded. She regained her steadiness slowly and looked up into Marc's face.

"Did you see what's in those cases?" she said between sobs. "I wasn't prepared to see all those grotesque things, those. . .those. . .human body parts. Those are the body parts of all the women he killed and mutilated. He kept them all to put in this macabre museum. There are no male parts, just females, and now I realize how terribly insane he is. Faces, genital lips, breast nipples, and all those other parts, even their uteruses are here. He even has the names of the women on museum tags. Please, Marc, let's get away from here. Take me out of this horrible place."

"I'm sorry you had to see all that, it's absolutely sickening." He pulled her behind him and helped her walk back out the door.

Marc opened what he thought was a closet only to find another whole room that housed half a dozen four-tier file cabinets. In front of them were two large worktables for laying out papers and maps, and several large holders of pens, pencils and painting brushes.

"So this is his work room where he does all his strategic planning," Marc mused.

"He must be a genius, Marc, but at the same time his mind is so terribly twisted and insane," Erika said emphatically.

"Yes, but it's all mixed together in his head," Marc said, "the pathology and the extremes of sheer talent, not to mention how fast his mind moves. At times in his life, he must have had some really tragic events that left him scarred forever. Most likely, those events involved his mother and father, and all the women who tried to get away from him. Now all he thinks about is hatred in general, but toward all women."

"Remember what Interpol told us," Marc added, "he was suspected of murdering and carving up almost a dozen women, but his methods don't exhibit the same kinds of activities that a serial killer's does. His methods don't fit the pattern of a true serial killer. That's where the insanity comes in – he's a collector of mutilated women."

Later, Marc found a stairway leading down to a lower floor. "C'mon, Erika, let's see what's down here." He took her hand and led her down the stairs. Arriving at the bottom, they pushed a light switch and a large room was immediately flooded with lights. From one end of the room to another, at least a half-dozen surgical tables were arranged two by two. Each set of tables was accompanied by carts revealing an extended operating room. Medical instruments and electronic diagnostic and surgical instruments lined the walls that had posters and charts fixed to the walls.

"Any hospital in the world would give a fortune to own equipment like this," Erika said. "He probably could do almost any kind of surgery."

Off in a corner, they came across Miss Worthington's dead body that had been surgically opened up and mutilated. Erika and Marc both had to look away from the grotesque scene. A tear rolled slowly down Erika's cheek. "Oh, Marc, what that poor woman went through. I hope she died quickly; we can't ever let Bill come across this."

"I'll get a couple of medics down here to remove her body," Marc promised.

Without warning, a hidden panel along the wall popped open revealing Lambert standing inside it holding a pistol and a knife. His face looked like it was made of wax as he stared first at Erika then at Marc. Moving quickly, he stepped behind Erika putting a large knife against her body and stuffing his pistol in the back of his belt.

"No, no, don't move an inch," he growled, "either one of you. It's so nice of you to visit my home. Now you're going to help me escape from this charade. Marc, drop the radio and your gun. DO IT NOW," Lambert shouted, "or so help me I'll gut her right here where she stands. You know I'll do it."

"Take it easy, Lambert," Marc spoke softly, bending over and putting his radio and pistol on the floor. "She's not going to hurt you like all those other women did – like your mother did. You don't have to think about all of them anymore, they're all in the past and you're here in the future. Let go of it, Gustav, it's over, finished."

"How would you know anything about them?" Lambert shot back. "Come stand in front of her and turn toward the door, we're all going out the door and get into a gondola. Don't even twitch, Marc, or she's dead. Now get moving!"

Outside the building, the trio encountered a soldier. "Don't even think about it," Lambert said. "This is a trench knife at her side – one false move out of anybody and it'll go right into her kidney and spleen. You soldiers there, get out of the way!"

Slowly, they walked toward the gondola, opened its doorway and stepped inside, Marc at one end of the gondola and Erika and Lambert at the other end.

"I told you a long time ago you'd never catch me, and you haven't caught me yet – I'm still in control." Lambert reached over with his free hand, engaging the motor controls that sent the gondola downward with a small jerking motion. He seemed much older than Marc imagined him to be, but his reflexes certainly were quick enough. Erika stood completely quiet without saying a word.

"Your bitch has a nice body, I can feel it through her clothes," Lambert grinned, "just like Simmons' secretary. She barely whimpered when I worked on her with a scalpel." He moved his free hand over her thigh and then up to her breasts. "I looked forward so much to exploring her body with my scalpel and adding some of her body parts to my exquisite museum which you just visited.

Pilatus cable gondola

I congratulate you, Erika, you're not even trembling. That's remarkable, especially since you're about to die. I bet you were really something in Marc's bed – young, fresh, soft and warm. Did you enjoy her, Marc, like I'm going to enjoy her?"

"No, you're about to die, you simple-minded fool!" Erika said forcefully. "This is the end of the road for you. It's payback time for all those women you murdered and cut up."

"Such a display of anger, Marc," Lambert teased, "I thought you police types were a little more under control."

"I am," Marc said, "and when I get the chance, you'll see how controlled I am. Don't think for a minute you're going to get out of this. By the time we get to the bottom, you'll wish you had a way to escape. Tell me, Lambert, do you think your mother would be so proud of you if she knew what you've done?"

"She would never know what I've done," Lambert responded, "and she wouldn't believe it, anyway. I used to sleep in bed with her and she let me play with her hair; the hair between her legs, I mean, and she kissed me everywhere on my body and I kissed her, too. Then she betrayed me and took herself away from me by hanging herself. After that, I hated her just like I hate all women; they're all alike with their empty promises."

What happened next took place so quickly it defied description. In what seemed like one single motion, Erika suddenly bent over forward at her waist with a closed fist and hit Lambert as hard as she could between his legs. Surprised and in pain, he dropped the knife; Erika quickly retrieved it and ran to the other end of the gondola beside Marc. Reaching behind his back, Lambert tried to pull the pistol from his belt.

The gondola swung forward, throwing Lambert still more off balance. Taking advantage of the moment, Marc jumped the short distance between them and hit him full force, throwing him more off balance and sending him against one of the glass windows, shattering it. Dozens of shards of glass littered the floor.

Marc and Lambert scuffled for a while, throwing themselves back and forth the length of the gondola. Both men began bleeding from their noses and mouths. Several heavy blows from Marc sent Lambert reeling backward and over the open edge of the broken window. With almost superhuman strength, Lambert grabbed the edge of the window from outside the gondola holding on for dear life. Despite his precarious position, he grabbed the edge of the now-open window. He held on as best he could while his hands began to bleed from the broken pieces of glass still left in the window.

"You're not going to let me fall, are you Marc? That's not the way the game is played. Help me back inside, or I'll cheat the hangman. You wouldn't want to do that, would you Marc? Hurry, I'm losing my grip."

Marc stood quietly by letting Lambert dangle outside the moving carriage a few moments, then reached over the side to grab the man's wrist. The cold mountain air swept in and out of the gondola. Marc stared out the open window of the gondola at the steep sides of the mountains while Lambert continued to reach for the pistol stuffed in his belt behind him. He proved too heavy for Marc to hold on to.

"Hurry, I'm slipping, I'm going to fall." With all his strength, Marc tried to pull him up but to no avail. Lambert began to kick his legs and twist and turn. "The air is so cold out here, my hands are freezing. Do you hate me so much you won't save me?"

"Yes, I hate you that much," Marc said. "You're a psychopath, Lambert, a sick, twisted, murdering son of a bitch without a conscience or any attempt at remorse. I hope all those women you cut up were dead before you began whittling on them."

"Some were and some weren't, but they still gave themselves to me," Lambert smiled. "Can you imagine what it felt like to have sex with a woman at the exact moment of death? It's absolutely indescribable."

"Move your other hand and hold on to me with both hands," Marc urged.

"I. . .I can't, the blood, I'm slipping away," Lambert begged. The look on his face was a mixture of anger and helplessness, and with that his hands slipped slowly out of Marc's, letting him go and plummeting downward toward the sharp, gnarled rocks below.

"Too bad," Marc was disappointed. "He's going to fall seven thousand feet to his death, poor soul. What a way to die. We'll get the soldiers to collect his body and bring it back."

Erika wiped the blood from Marc's face and hands. "I can't say I'm sorry to see it all end this way," Erika confided. "He was the worst kind of human being this planet could possibly produce. His grisly life was nothing but anger and hatred and twisted revenge; the world is so much better off without him."

"At sometime in life, a man has to decide what kind of person he wants to be," Marc said, "and then he has to become that person. We all have a choice. We must be willing – at a moment's notice – to give up who we are in order to become who we might be – a person of substance and great value to the human race. I don't know who first said that, but it's one of life's most fundamental driving forces. Lambert just was forced to make all the wrong choices."

They held onto each other as the gondola made it's slow descent. "That poor man, slashing out against everything and everyone," Erika said. "All he knew to do was to hate the world and everyone in it. What a terrible life he must have had. Really, he didn't have any kind of life at all, only darkness and flailing against his own hurt. There were no beautiful sunsets, no days of laughter and sharing of good times. It's just unimaginable."

Epilogue

Marc reached out his hand and put it on Simmons' shoulder in a gesture of sincere sympathy.

"I'm so very sorry about your secretary, Bill, I know you must have loved each other a great deal. Many of us share your sacrifice and your heartache, you aren't alone."

Simmons coughed slightly and, in true British fashion, turned to look out the window. "At least we were together for almost a year," he said quietly. "I'll remember this saga for the rest of my life. I'm only sorry we couldn't bring Lambert to trial. I wanted so much to see him swinging on the gallows. He destroyed everything he touched in a terrible rage against humanity that he couldn't control."

"We all wanted to see him swing at the end of the executioner's rope, Bill," Marc said. "Of all the really despicable criminals I've known during my short lifetime, he more than any deserved to swing at the end of the hangman's rope. But at least his gang was completely destroyed, and we know for certain he's dead and can't harm society any longer."

The week following the attack on Lambert's Mount Pilatus stronghold was filled with the arrests and convictions of all known immediate gang members. During the attack, twelve British

Airborne commandos were lost along with twenty-one wounded. In addition, eight more American 82nd Airborne troops were killed with fourteen wounded, and four Scotland Yard officers were killed along with six more wounded. In all the history of law enforcement, the destruction of the international Lambert gang still ranks as the most far-reaching and closely integrated operation ever mounted against one criminal group.

"Would you like to see the televised newsreel announcement of the capture of the gang and it's leader?" Simmons offered.

"I guess so," Erika said.

Simmons turned on the tele and CD player, and set the program to play.

"This announcement was aired on TV in fourteen European countries and three American stations in New York, Missouri and Washington D.C.," Simmons said.

> On the international scene, a joint statement today by the American Federal Bureau of Investigation and authorities in the British Scotland Yard, announced the capture and incarceration of ninety-eight members of the Lambert International Gang of thieves and smugglers.
>
> Scotland Yard Chief Inspector William Simmons commented that the capture of so large a group of European criminals was the result of close strategic cooperation between law enforcement agents in numerous countries. The multi-national sweep of criminals represents a high watermark in the annals of all law enforcement agencies involved.
>
> 'Gustav Blaatner', the leader of the gang, was known by the alias 'Mr. Lambert'. His body was identified by authorities after he fell from a gondola

car returning from Mount Pilatus outside Lucerne, Switzerland. The Lambert Gang was responsible for thefts of weapons, drugs, paintings, and operations involving the trade in human trafficking, it was made known today. Blaatner, known as 'Mr. Lambert', was buried where he fell. The British Geographic Society has decided to label all their maps where the leader fell as 'Lambert's Fall'.

In local news today. . .

"Well, that's nice of the Geographic Society to mark the spot with *Lambert's Fall* on all their maps," Erika chuckled.

Simmons, Barker, Marc and Erika said their goodbyes with hugs and well wishing, and left to go their own ways. For all of them, it seemed like the end of an era in their lives. Erika and Marc packed their suitcases and headed for Tenby, their forever secret hideaway.

★ ★ ★

At Tenby, Marc and Erika sat at dinner in their favorite restaurant by the sea, watching the sun set over the harbor.

"I feel so at peace here," Erika said, "watching the sunset and just being with you, and knowing that terrible ordeal is over. It will be quite some time before this horrible ordeal will fade from my consciousness."

"I, too, feel at peace here, far from the reality of a world that some of us feel a need to protect society from," Marc responded. "It's almost as if the past several months are some kind of bad dream, a nightmare even. But it's over now and we'll never have to go through it again." They both fell silent for a moment. Marc reached over and squeezed her hand.

"Honey, I haven't had time to tell you this, we've been so busy," Marc said.

"Oh, dear, what's happened now?" Erika looked across the table at him. "You're not going to make me cry in my soup, are you?"

"It seems the St. Louis County Council has offered me a job as Chief of Police at Manchester, with quite a large raise in salary. Chief Warner is retiring at the end of the month. What do you think of that?"

"Oh, I guess it's your choice," Erika said sniffling a little. "Do you really want to go back to St. Louis and chase after robbers and hold-up men?"

Marc looked at her face for a long time. He could tell she was disappointed by the way she looked down at the center of the table, then suddenly grew silent.

"No, it's OUR choice, love, and I have an idea," Marc said suddenly, taking note of the time on his watch.

"Oh, oh, so do I," Erika said, and they both stood up at the same time.

"We've explored Tenby pretty much," Marc said thoughtfully, "but we never went inside the church. It's a quaint old building not very far from here, and it's where a man named Robert Recorde invented the equal sign in mathematics. He was a busy guy, court physician to King Edward VI.

"Where did you find out all this about a mathematician?" Erika queried. "I didn't know you were interested in mathematics."

Marc smiled at her quizzically. "I could care less about mathematics right now; I'm more interested in the church."

"You never told me your decision about St. Louis and Chief of police," she reminded him. "Don't you think at least we should talk about it? Okay, let's go see this 'quaint' old church," she said resolutely with a sigh, "how do we get there?"

After a bit of a walk, they came to the church and stood in front of it, looking up at the tall spire and the beautiful stained glass windows.

"Listen, somebody's playing the organ, isn't it beautiful?" Erika said.

Marc took her hand and together they went inside. Erika leaned against Marc when she realized what she was seeing. At the front of the church were FBI Special Agent Dobson, Scotland Yard Chief Inspector William Simmons, Assistant Scotland Yard Chief Inspector James Barker, and Colonel Ted Richards of the 82nd Airborne Division. Their wives also were there, seated in the front pews.

Erika turned and scowled at Marc, then began slapping his shoulder.

Church at Tenby, Wales

"How did you arrange all this," she howled, "how did you do it without me knowing about it? You naughty little boy, and I don't even have a wedding dress."

"Well. . ." Marc stammered, "this isn't all of it. There's more."

Erika's jaw dropped as she looked around the room. "How could there be more. . .more of what?"

"I'll show you a little later," Marc confided to her, "but if you stand up inside the steeple and look out at the harbor, there's a little house high up on the hill behind the buildings. It's our house, I bought it just for us, our forever secret hideaway, and we can live there forever if we want to. How does that sound?"

She squinted at him for a few seconds, then quietly said between her teeth, "And I suppose you even slipped away and bought a wedding ring!"

"Well, no," Marc said with a laugh, "we're going to have to use this cigar band until we can get a ring." Marc retrieved a beautiful engagement ring from his pocket along with a diamond wedding ring.

Erika wheeled around and shouted down the aisle, "You sneaky police types are all alike, and you were all in this together, weren't you? And I love you all for what you've done."

The priest finally wailed with a Welsh brogue, "And I'm supposed to promise and guarantee that you two will live happily ever after, is that it? Now, can we get on with this, I haven't even had dinner yet."

"Yes, we're going to be late for the reception!" Marc laughed.

Suddenly Erika stopped halfway down the aisle and turned full forward in front of Marc. "Well. . .what did you tell St. Louis?"

Looking very solemn and downcast, then he suddenly smiled. "I turned down the job." Erika threw her arms around Marc's neck and kissed him several times, jumping up and down. "I love you, I love, I love you," Erika said excitedly.

"Hey," Marc said, "wait a minute, we haven't even got to the altar yet."